After being woken by a phone call in the middle of the night by his alpha, Leopold Caldwell heads to San Francisco. Alpha Declan requests his services in creating an identity for a rescued human whore. What Leo finds when he gets there is a scared young human who is completely overwhelmed by his new reality. Oh, and he happens to be Leo's mate. Even as he's ecstatic to meet Jerry, the other half of his soul, Leo recognizes the hurdles they're facing. Not only is Jerry struggling to accept the existence of shifters, but there are also still people after him . . . people who seem bent on establishing possession of Jerry. After a close call where Jerry is nearly kidnapped, Leo decides it's time for a change of scenery. He takes him back to Stone Ridge and a secluded cabin owned by his family line. Unfortunately, trouble follows. Can Leo use his quick wit swiftly enough to save not only Jerry but his own future as well?

With a Wolf's Support
Copyright © 2019 Charlie Richards
ISBN: 978-1-4874-2431-2
Cover art by Angela Waters

Published by eXtasy Books Inc or
Devine Destinies, an imprint of eXtasy Books Inc

Look for us online at:
www.eXtasybooks.com or www.devinedestinies.com

With a Wolf's Support
Wolves of Stone Ridge Book 47

By

Charlie Richards

DEDICATION

Minds are like flowers, they only open when the time is right.
~Unknown

CHAPTER ONE

Leopold Caldwell didn't know when he'd managed to fall into an uneasy sleep. When the trill of his cell phone yanked him back to wakefulness, he hissed as pain spiked through his neck. He really shouldn't have fallen asleep in that chair.

"Ow," he grumbled under his breath as he rubbed the back of his neck.

Then the sound of his phone caught his attention again, and he recalled why he'd been sitting in the uncomfortable chair to begin with. His cousin's daughter, Stephani, had been kidnapped, along with his alpha's daughter, Sara. His cousin and his partner—Luther and Deke—had traveled to San Francisco with Alpha Declan and a myriad of others from the pack in order to track them down and rescue them.

Leo had wanted to go, but there hadn't been room in the helicopter. Instead, he'd been left behind, his wolf chuffing with annoyance in the back of his mind, while he waited impatiently for information. Hence falling asleep on the un-comfortable piece of furniture as he'd been waiting for word.

"This is Leo," he barked into the phone as soon as he con-nected the call, not even bothering to check the caller ID.

"I've sent Manon to get you," Alpha Declan stated, the alpha wolf shifter's voice coming through the line. "I have a young man here who needs a new identity once he's rational enough to decide on what he wants . . . and that shifters ex-ist."

"He knows about shifters?" The words were out of Leo's

mouth before he could stop himself. While he was curious, it wasn't the most pressing issue. "How are Stephani and Sara? Are they okay?"

Alpha Declan's deep, tired sigh came through the line loud and clear. The simple action betrayed that their pack leader wasn't invincible after all. The man had to be exhausted after everything he must have gone through—not only had it been his daughter kidnapped, but he would have had to console his mate while keeping it together enough to plan the rescue.

So glad I'm not in his shoes.

"Sara is a little banged up, but she'll be fine, in time"—a growl entered Declan's tone as he added—"as long as her mate gets his head out of his ass, anyway."

Leo's jaw sagged open, and he knew his eyes widened. Before he could question the alpha on that statement, however, his alpha continued.

"I'm sorry to say that Stephani came out a little worse for wear. She was injured protecting Sara, and she's still unconscious."

Upon hearing that, Leo felt his heart rate spike.

His sweet, feisty, dominant cousin was injured.

Leo guessed he must have made some noise betraying his distress, for Alpha Declan rumbled, "Take a few slow deep breaths, Leopold. Lark is with her and feels that she'll wake up soon. She may even be mostly well by the time ye get here."

Doing as he'd been bidden, Leo took a few slow, deep breaths. The spots that he hadn't even realized had been dancing before his eyes disappeared.

Yeah, breathing is a good thing.

"Right, right," Leo mumbled when he had the breath. He cleared his throat before adding, "So, when should I be at Manon's private helipad?"

Leo figured some of the documents for the wolf enforcer

to build a private landing pad at his place in the woods had probably been forged, but he wasn't one to judge. As one of the pack's lawyers, he helped by forging personal documents all the time. Since paranormals lived for centuries and needed to hide from the general human populace, coupled with the advancement of technology, shifters had to have their identities reinvented every few decades.

Having always been technologically inclined, Leo helped with that.

"Ye have three hours," Alpha Declan told him. "That'll give ye time to pull any information ye can find on Jerry De Mara's past. Family, friends, as much as ye can. He claims not to have anyone looking for him. Jerry doesn't smell as if he's lying, but after the scare Luther put in him, well . . . I'd like to be sure."

Leo's brows shot up. "Luther scared him? How?" His cousin was usually a fairly relaxed wolf. Of course, finding his daughter injured could most certainly change that.

"Jerry led us to the room where our girls were, and we rushed inside. Jerry followed, but he was closest to the door." Declan scoffed softly, and Leo imagined his wry smile. "We were checking the girls when Jerry squeaked, drawing our attention. A gorilla of a man was standing in the doorway pointing a gun at Stephani, maybe because she was already injured. When the asshole stated, *lie on the floor, or I'll finish what my buddy started*, Luther understandably lost it. He shifted faster than I'd ever seen him and tore the man apart."

Wincing, Leo nodded absently. He could totally see his cousin doing that. Hell, if Leo had been there instead, he would have done the same.

"So . . ." Leo drew the word out. "How did he take it?"

"Well, Jerry didn't piss himself, so I'll give him props for that," Declan replied dryly. "He seemed a bit catatonic after that, though. Lark hasn't been able to see to him, yet, but I'm sure I'll have more for ye by the time ye arrive."

Checking his watch, Leo nodded absently. "Yes, Alpha. I'll see what I can find out about Jerry, then be at Manon's at quarter after midnight."

"Good. I'll see ye soon, then."

When Alpha Declan disconnected the call without another word, Leo didn't feel offended. He knew his alpha had to have a lot on his plate right about then. Instead, Leo shoved to his feet, strode out of the living area, and headed to his bedroom.

Within ten minutes, Leo had his duffel bag packed as well as a garment bag containing a suit. He liked to be prepared. After a quick shower to clear the last of the sleep from his mind, Leo dressed in comfortable blue jeans, a dark-green polo shirt, and worn, dark-brown cowboy boots.

Seeing he still had almost two hours before he needed to hop in his truck, Leo made a detour to his kitchen for a bottle of water before he headed to his office. He booted up his laptop. After completing the obvious search—typing Jerry De Mara into the *Google* search engine—Leo stared at the single entry that popped up. It was an announcement for the winner of a spelling bee.

Leo clicked on the link and swiftly skimmed the article.

He won a spelling bee when he was eleven years old. Huh.

Taking a look at the picture, Leo couldn't help but smile. The wide grin stretched the boy's face, and even in the black and white picture, he could see the joy lighting his eyes. To his surprise, he even felt a whine of interest from his wolf.

So weird.

It almost felt as if his animal wanted to lick the boy all over and protect the human from all the dangers of the world.

Leo could think of only a few people that had roused that reaction, and they had all been family.

Pushing the reaction to the back of his mind for later perusal, Leo continued his search. He pulled the school's records, which was located two hours north of San Francisco. After careful review, he noticed that Jerry made top grades and appeared to be a model student.

Jerry had extra-curricular activities that ranged from soccer to 4-H. In eighth grade, there was a picture of him resting his hand on the back of a hog while holding a blue ribbon with his other. The following year, Jerry sat on the back of a horse, decked out for roping, and the caption read — *Jerry De Mara, second place county high school rodeo champion.*

Everything Leo found pointed to the fact that Jerry dedicated his energy one hundred percent to everything he set his mind to.

So why did he suddenly drop out of school at age fifteen?

Leo's gut clenched, and he sucked in a harsh breath.

Fifteen. Tenth grade. Hormones. Body changes. Where he ended up . . .

All the possibilities swirled through Leo's mind, but he didn't want to jump to conclusions. He moved his search to information on Jerry's family. The human had a brother, younger by three years, and according to property records, their parents still resided in the same house. With a deep sigh, Leo used a few tricks to get into tax records . . . and he grimaced at what he found.

Not only did the parents stop claiming two dependents that same year, but their charitable donation deductions were listed to an organization some considered more cult than church.

"Well, hell," Leo muttered. "That's a damn shame."

Did Jerry leave on his own because he knew he was different? Or was he forced out?

Leo had every intention of finding out. A glance toward his watch told him he still had twenty minutes before he needed to leave. His grumbling stomach told him how he should spend that time.

Leo tightened his leather trench coat around himself, shoving his hands into his pockets. He squinted against the wind as he watched the helicopter land on the pad which was situated over a hundred yards behind Manon's home. Hunching his shoulders, he did his best to ignore the chill.

A few seconds after the whirly-bird had landed, the whine of the engine softened, and the rotors began to slow. He watched the door open, and Manon slipped out, ducking under the still-churning blades. The wolf shifter enforcer jogged toward him, nodding in greeting.

"Give me ten minutes. I gotta run in and piss, then grab a sandwich and water. Stow your stuff and strap it down, will ya?" Then he winked and added, "Also gonna kiss my man and tell him how much I miss him."

Leo was still nodding when Manon disappeared down the trail.

"Stow my stuff," Leo muttered under his breath. He'd never been in a helicopter but still. "How hard could it be?"

Leo took his time figuring it out.

To Leo's surprise, he enjoyed his first helicopter ride. With his superior shifter eyesight, even though it was night, he could make out quite a bit of what was below them. The sensation of soaring through the air was almost as enjoyable as running through the forest in wolf form—almost.

"I see why you learned how to fly one of these," Leo called over the rumble of the engine. "This is fun."

Manon glanced his way for an instant before returning his focus to the controls. "Yep. Did Alpha Declan fill you in?"

Leo nodded. "For the most part."

"Good." Manon chuckled darkly. "That way we don't have to shout back and forth the whole ride."

Laughing, Leo returned his focus to the darkness outside.

They reached the airport a little after three in the morning. As Leo relaxed in the passenger seat of the SUV that Manon drove — he'd offered, but the enforcer had told him it would be easier for him to drive since he knew the way — he noticed the illuminated bank sign reading two-twelve AM.

Right. We gained an hour.

They drove through surprisingly still-crowded streets. Cars honked, tires squealed, and the music from other vehicles thumped as they passed them. That was something Leo sure didn't miss. Living in the country offered a much quieter, sedate lifestyle that, as a wolf shifter, Leo craved.

And a mate.

Leo had been watching all his friends, and even his family, find their mates for years. At almost two hundred years old, he would love to finally find someone to call his own. His patience was wearing thin, so he sure hoped Fate hurried the fuck up.

"Wow, nice houses," Leo commented, staring out the window and admiring the mansions, hoping to distract himself from his wayward thoughts.

"Well, as it turns out, Jared refuses to stay in anything but the finest." Manon smiled wryly as he glanced Leo's way. "And of course Carson isn't going to do a damn thing to counter his mate."

Laughing softly, Leo murmured, "Yeah."

Leo didn't spend a lot of time with most of the wolves of the inner circle. With his duties of monitoring the length of time the adults in their pack had lived as a certain identity, he spent a lot of time with everyone else in the pack. In the past, Leo had sent his reports, which contained his recommendations of who should soon consider a change, to Beta Shane Alvaro.

Since Beta Shane had moved on to take a position on the

Shifter Council, Leo had begun sending the reports to Alpha Declan himself. Even though they'd held a challenge—which was won by a big, dominant, blond wolf shifter named Dixon Holsteen—so a new beta had been assigned, Leo hadn't yet been given the word to send the reports to him. From what Leo had heard, Alpha Declan was still easing him into his myriad of duties.

One of those would eventually be working with Leo to coordinate with the shifters in their pack to change their identities. In order to do that, however, Dixon had to know everyone in the pack. He had to meet them, learn about who they were, how long they'd been in the pack, and absorb the complexity of their relationships around them.

Seeing as Leo already knew the information, he didn't envy Dixon the process.

It was a lot to take in.

The same as nearly everyone in the pack who could get the day off of work, Leo had been at the Right for Position challenge. He'd seen the dominant shifters fight. It'd been damn impressive, and Leo had been glad he would never be pitted against any of them—gods willing. While his wolf was fairly dominant, it took a certain aggressiveness to want to fight for a top position.

Leo just didn't have it.

"This is it." Manon's voice cut into Leo's thoughts. "You awake over there?"

Jerking his focus back to the wolf enforcer, Leo took in the lines of tension etched on Manon's face. "I'm awake. Was just lost in thought," he admitted, turning his attention to the house—mansion—they were approaching. "Took a nap earlier," he admitted. "Now I'm ready to check on my family before finding a bed. I bet you're ready to crash, though."

"You know it."

The gate opened before them, and Manon steered the vehicle down the long driveway and past gorgeous landscaping. Leo spotted the house and found himself smirking. When Carson's mate said he wanted nice digs to rescue people and take out some drug gangs, he wasn't kidding. Of course, Leo had to admit that since they were within a fenced estate, it had to help with safety, too.

As their vehicle approached, the garage door on the far-left side opened. Manon parked them inside the cavernous space. Once the other shifter turned off the engine, Leo pushed out of the vehicle, closing the door behind him. He opened the back door and grabbed his bags. After slinging his suit bag over his shoulder, Leo used his hip to close the door, then he followed Manon across the garage toward a door on the far end.

Manon used a key to unlock it, then opened it and led the way inside.

Leo stepped into a large foyer and waited as Manon closed and locked the door behind him. Following the other shifter once more, he was led through a back hallway. He pointed toward the far end, explaining that it led to a back foyer.

"Here's the main hall," Manon murmured softly, opening a door and stepping through. He pointed toward the stairs to the right, saying, "I'm supposed to take you to Alpha Declan first, though. He said he'd still be up."

Even as Leo nodded, a scent tickled his senses, distracting him. He turned to the left as he inhaled more deeply. A mossy, earthy fragrance somehow mixed with a natural male aroma. It left his taste buds tingling and his mouth watering.

Needing to discern the source, Leo set his bags down on a nearby settee. While he figured it was a piece of furniture that was probably only for decoration, Leo didn't care. Parsing out the source of the exquisite aroma . . . that was all that mattered.

"Leo?" Manon called. "Where are you going?"

"I need—" Leo glanced over his shoulder and spotted Manon's questioning expression. "What's this way?"

"The kitchen and dining areas."

Nodding absently, Leo picked up his pace. Anticipation flooded him, and his breathing quickened. Even his wolf grew excited in his mind.

Leo pushed open a door and peered around, taking in a small, dark dining room. His keen eyesight surveyed a bar separating the space, which led into a huge kitchen. His gaze fixated on a young man standing frozen before the open door of the refrigerator, his form silhouetted in the light.

Sucking in a harsh breath, Leo could only stare. The human was, in a word, stunning. He appeared lean—easily seen even hidden beneath a pair of loose-fitting sleep pants and a t-shirt—and stood perhaps five-foot-eight or nine. *I'll have to get closer to be sure.* His hair gleamed red in the light of the refrigerator, wild and unkempt.

Even while admiring all that, Leo noticed the male's wide, wide green eyes . . . eyes full of trepidation and fear.

Why? What's wrong?

Leo longed to soothe the man, and the reason why hit him hard.

He's my mate!

Leo swallowed convulsively, forcing moisture into his mouth. "Damn. Fate listened," he whispered.

Manon lifted a brow, his expression one of confusion. "What are you talking about?"

Unable to tear his gaze away from the svelte, red-haired figure staring at them with that wide-eyed, fearful look, Leo felt another stab of need to ease the tension filling the human's frame. "He's my mate."

Chapter Two

Shit! How did I miss that someone other than these guys's leader was still up?

Jerry De Mara had been listening for hours until the house had fallen quiet. True, it was a big ass house, but he'd been so sure . . . well, all except the big Native American guy and his small, hazel-eyed partner. Jerry couldn't remember their names, but he knew they liked loud sex.

His own prick had begun to thicken when he'd heard the sounds they were making. That was what had finally driven him from his room. The grumbling of his stomach was a good instigator, too.

Standing before the open refrigerator, trying to decide what he could sneak without someone noticing, he felt grateful the cool air caused his semi to go down.

The opening of the nearby dining room door sent fear spiking through him. The view of the gorgeous specimen of maleness twisted his stomach further, filling it with butterflies. His belly fluttered, and his heart felt as if it skipped a beat.

Oh my goodness!

Jerry gaped at the man, staring. He couldn't tear his gaze away. From what he could see in the dim lighting, the man sported ruggedly handsome good looks, and Jerry wanted to see more.

Then another man appeared behind the stranger . . . one Jerry recognized, snapping his attention back to the present — Manon Lemelle — a wolf shifter.

Oh, I am so busted.

Jerry's mind whirled, making him miss whatever exchange was whispered between the stranger and Manon.

"I'll let Alpha Declan know we've arrived," Manon stated, his voice louder. He grinned widely at the other man, slapping him on the back. Then he nodded at Jerry, still smiling, before slipping out the door.

"Hi," the stranger said, drawing Jerry's attention back to him. He stood on the other side of the bar, his left forearm resting on it. Holding his right hand over the counter toward him, he continued, "Jerry, right?"

Releasing the hold he had on the refrigerator door, Jerry nodded as he reached out and took the man's hand. He let out a small gasp as tingles sparked over his palm, causing goose bumps to erupt on his forearm. His instinct was to yank his hand away, but the stranger's hold tightened a bit, staying that action.

"Hi, Jerry. I'm Leopold Caldwell." With only the moonlight streaming through the window to illuminate him, the man's eyes appeared to glimmer in the darkness. "Please call me Leo. It's very nice to meet you."

Jerry heard the warmth in Leo's tone and wondered from where it stemmed. Then it hit him. "Caldwell," he murmured. "Um, related to Stephani?"

Leo nodded. "She's my cousin's daughter. Luther is my father's sister's son." He winked. "My cousin."

Sucking in a harsh breath, Jerry finally yanked his hand away. "C-Cousin? That m-means you're, uh, you're, um—"

He couldn't manage to finish the thought.

Fortunately, Leo put him out of his misery. "A shifter? Yeah. Wolf, like him." He leaned over and flipped a light switch, and the drop lighting over the bar cast the area in soft illumination. "Keep breathing, cutie. Please? None of us here will hurt you."

Jerry nodded slowly and focused on the countertop.

"One breath at a time," Leo continued, his deep soothing croon sounding directly in Jerry's ear. "That's the way."

When did Leo round the counter? How did I miss him drawing so close?

Even as Jerry flinched from Leo's touch, he took comfort in the sound of his voice. He managed to slow his breathing. When Leo rested his palm on Jerry's back a second time, he pressed into the touch, and his tension eased.

"That's the way, Jerry," Leo purred into his ear. "We're actually a pretty nice group. Luther was just protecting Stephani, that's all."

Jerry nodded. It had been explained to him. That didn't make the memory any less scary . . . or the fact that shifters were real any easier to swallow, either. There were creatures out there that could tear him apart with ease.

Of course, the gangsters that had been running his life for the last nearly six years could do the same thing.

Was it any different?

Probably not. They're both wolves . . . just of a different sort.

Dismissing the strange thought, Jerry cast a side-eyed glance at the handsome man offering him comfort. With the light on and without the bar between them, he could finally make out the rest of his features. The guy cut a fine figure, to say the least.

Leo stood a good five inches taller than Jerry's own five-foot-eight-inch frame. He was broader with a trimmed waist and plenty of wiry strength in his frame. His hazel eyes held an unexpected warmth, and Jerry thought Leo had a kind, strong face.

His muscular legs were encased in worn, comfortable-looking jeans. He had a brown leather jacket hiding his wide-shouldered torso. Even the man's dark-blond hair, which appeared to be finger-combed rather than styled, looked fantastic on the guy.

Geez. How does a guy look that good without appearing to even be trying . . . and in the middle of the night?

For the first time in nearly five years, Jerry felt the stirrings of arousal . . . and his groin heated as his blood flowed south. He relished the sensation for several heartbeats. While he'd gotten off with some of the johns he'd serviced over the years, he'd never been aroused *before* their dick had repeatedly pegged his gland, forcing his body to respond. Getting turned on by the sounds of two hot men fucking totally didn't count. These sensations—the heat and desire—was specific . . . a yearning for a particular person.

Jerry had wondered if he could still find a man attractive.

Unable to help himself, Jerry glanced down at Leo's fly. There was an impressive bulge behind the man's zipper. Jerry's mouth watered, wondering what the man's jeans were hiding.

His dick actually twitched at the thought.

Which reminded Jerry of his own state of dress—a pair of thin sleep pants and a t-shirt.

Shit!

Jerry cleared his throat and attempted to turn left, so he was again facing the refrigerator. It would also work to hide his arousal from the man. Plus, if he could get the door open, maybe the coolness would help ease him.

Although, unlike before, where Jerry had found a few sounds of males enjoying themselves hot and could walk away from them, right then, the object of his desire stood nearby. Leo was so masculine. He was a little hard to ignore.

"Hey, do they have bottled water in there?" Leo asked, stepping back. "It was a long flight. Ever been on a helicopter, Jerry?"

Reaching into the refrigerator, Jerry grabbed a bottle of water. The confusion he felt about Leo's sudden shift in conversation did more to help ease his arousal than the cold, but whatever worked. Half turning, he handed the bottle to the man, careful to keep from touching him again.

Leo's touch was just too enticing, making him want things that he couldn't possibly have. No way would the handsome man be interested in a used-up whore like him.

Jerry focused on the question. "No." He turned back to the fridge and grabbed a bottle of water for himself, just to keep his hands occupied. He twisted off the lid and chugged a few gulps.

"First time for me, too," Leo replied, his voice warm and animated. He didn't seem put off at all by Jerry's curt response. "Have you ever wanted to ride in one? After enjoying the flight with Manon, I just may have to take lessons."

Jerry turned and peered at Leo, meeting his gaze fully. Seeing the open curiosity filling his expression as well as the smile curving his lips, his brain stalled. He couldn't figure out why Leo was interested.

Why isn't he asking me about the gangsters?

That was what all the other people wanted to know . . . or how long he'd been a whore, how he'd gotten in that line of work — as if he'd had a choice — and did he know anything about some guy named Larson.

Before Jerry could come up with a response — it had been a long time since he'd thought about any wishes he'd had for his life — his stomach growled.

Leo hummed. "Ah, Manon and I interrupted your midnight snack. Sorry about that." He grinned as he stepped closer and peered over Jerry's shoulder and into the fridge. "What did you plan on? Are you a sweet or salty kind of guy?"

"I-I . . ." Jerry began, then returned his focus to the contents of the refrigerator. There was leftover steak, yogurt cups, fruit salad in *Tupperware,* and so much more.

"And I bet . . . yeah." As Leo spoke, he crossed to a closed door to the left and opened it. "Score!"

Curiosity rising in him for the first time in what felt like forever, Jerry released the refrigerator door. As it swung closed, he headed toward Leo. The man must have noticed, for he flashed a wide grin Jerry's way over his shoulder, then stepped left while half-pivoting. With his right hand, Leo indicated inside the room.

Jerry gasped, and his eyes widened. The huge space could have been called a pantry . . . except it was three times bigger than any pantry that Jerry had ever seen. It had to be twelve by twenty-four feet, with shelf after shelf full of dry and canned goods. To the right, there were packages of cookies, canisters of nuts, and bags of chips.

Leo laughed as he wrapped his arm around Jerry's shoulders. Even though Jerry tensed, the big man still tucked him close and squeezed lightly. Then he eased his hand away from his upper arm, only to slide it toward the middle of his back and down his spine, sending a shiver through Jerry's nerve endings. When Leo's palm reached his lower back, he pressed lightly, urging him forward and through the doorway.

Jerry stepped away from Leo's palm and swung around, a cry escaping his lips as fear flooded him. The walls of the small room seemed to cave in around him. His mind flashed back to memories of being shoved into a dark space by not only nameless strangers but by his owners.

He just knew in the next instant that he would be shoved against one of the shelves, hard, and his sleep pants would be torn from him and —

"Hey, easy, Jer. You're okay. Deep breaths, little one. Deep breaths. One after another. You'll be fine. You're safe."

Doing as he'd been bidden, Jerry took a deep breath. He let it out, then took another one. A fresh, masculine scent tickled his senses. It was pleasant, so Jerry took another couple of breaths, wanting to enjoy it some more.

"There ya go. That's the way. Nothing will happen to you, Jerry. You have my word."

Just as Jerry realized that not only were trembles racking his body, he noticed the bands around his torso were Leo's arms . . . and they weren't holding him tightly. Leo cradled him loosely, rubbing his palms up and down his back. His touch was soothing and gentle, just like his words and tone. Everything about Leo was reassuring.

Oh, and it was Leo's scent that he was enjoying.

Or cologne, maybe? Because no way could someone smell that good naturally.

Shivering, Jerry dragged himself together. He grimaced, hating that he'd just had a mental freak-out in front of this obviously strong and confident man.

He must think I'm such a weak loser.

"Come on, Jer," Leo murmured, easing his right hand up his spine, so he could begin massaging his nape. He rested his other hand on Jerry's hip, rubbing the jutting bone through his t-shirt. "Meet my gaze, sweetheart. Let me see your pretty green eyes. I wanna know you're here with me."

Jerry tipped his chin up just enough to peer at Leo through his lashes. To his surprise, he didn't see censure or even pity. Instead, a wealth of concern and even understanding stared back at him.

Leo's lips curved up slightly at the edges. "There you are, Jer," he crooned softly as he brought the hand at his nape around to cradle his jaw. He used the hold to urge Jerry's chin up a bit more, so their gazes clashed more fully. "I'm sorry my actions triggered something uncomfortable for you." His brows drew together, and his expression turned pained. "Will you forgive me?"

Gaping, Jerry struggled to come up with a response. *Leo is asking for . . . for . . . forgiveness?* Jerry could barely process it. He couldn't remember the last time someone had apologized to him.

Long before . . .

No. I'm not going to think about them.

"Please, sweetheart?" Leo's cheeks took on a pinkish hue even as he added, "If you'd like to talk about . . . uh, whatever happened, I'm a great listener."

"I forgive you," Jerry blurted out. After all, how could he not? It wasn't Leo's fault that he was messed up in the head. Forcing a smile, he muttered, "It wasn't your fault. And I-I don't"—heaving a sigh, he wrapped his arms around his torso—"I don't want to talk about it."

Leo opened his mouth but paused. His brows were still furrowed, and for an instant, Jerry thought the man would push. Then his features eased into a warm smile.

"In that case, comfort food. Grab those ruffled potato chips." Leo pointed as he eased away, releasing him. "I saw chip dip in the fridge. And I'm going to make us some grilled turkey and cheese sandwiches." Taking a step backward, he winked while offering a roguish smile. "For dessert, *Oreos* and milk. What do you say?"

Jerry didn't have to answer. His stomach did it for him, giving a loud rumble. Hearing Leo's chuckle, he ducked his head, his cheeks heating.

"Sounds like your stomach likes the idea, at least," Leo commented, touching Jerry's jaw lightly with a crooked finger, then pointed toward a shelf. "Grab those double stuffed, right there, too. I'm gonna start cooking."

With those parting words, Leo turned and headed out of the pantry.

Jerry found his gaze straying down . . . down . . . and riveting on Leo's butt. The globes flexed beneath the faded denim, causing his mouth to water. Shaking his head at himself, Jerry grabbed the items Leo had mentioned and headed out of the pantry.

No way would a man like that want a tainted guy like me, but he sure is nice. Maybe these shifters aren't so bad after all.

Adult, Erotic Romance, Gay, GLBT, Paranormal, Shapeshifter

CHAPTER THREE

When Jerry had panicked in the pantry, Leo's heart had nearly pounded out of his chest. His wolf had whined in the back of his mind, and he'd nearly lost it. Only knowing his mate needed him calm had helped him keep his head.

He'd wanted to hunt down every bastard and john who'd ever hurt Jerry and make them pay . . . badly.

Instead, Leo had set those desires aside and used the opportunity to wrap his arms around Jerry. As he'd rubbed up and down his back and whispered words of encouragement, it had felt so damn good. Never in his wildest dreams had Leo imagined that simply holding another being would feel so amazing.

Too bad Leo couldn't just sweep Jerry into his arms and take him to the nearest free bedroom so they could explore what was between them. Even though he'd caught his mate breathing in his scent, which caused him to relax in his arms, Leo knew his human wouldn't understand. His skittish little mate would need time.

I can give him that. I've waited nearly two hundred years. I can give Jerry as much time as he needs.

Gods, at least, I hope I can.

Leo had always thought he'd had a pretty good amount of patience, but now he understood why shifters worked so hard to claim their mate as swiftly as possible. Finding a mate made everything different.

Shoulda listened to my cousin on that one.

Dismissing the random thought—like all the times he'd teased Luther when the man was stressing over convincing Deke to move in with him permanently—Leo headed to the refrigerator and began pulling out everything he would need to make grilled turkey and cheese sandwiches. He grabbed the butter, cheese slices, and turkey in one hand, then snagged the French onion dip in the other—that he placed on the bar counter before carrying the rest to the counter space to the left of the stove.

"Have a seat at the bar and enjoy some chips and dip, Jer," Leo encouraged as he watched Jerry sidle back into the kitchen. "There are napkins in the wooden holder against that wall there," he added, pointing, even as he noticed Jerry clutched the items that Leo had told him to grab to his chest, but he kept his gaze focused on the tile floor. Seeing that the slender male's posture screamed discomfort, Leo did his best to keep his smile relaxed and his body loose, non-combative and welcoming. "Snack away. I'll have these sandwiches whipped up in no time."

To Leo's pleasure, Jerry grabbed a couple of napkins, then settled on a bar stool near the dip Leo had placed there.

Less than ten minutes later, Leo carried two plates to the bar, placing one before Jerry and a second in front of an empty stool. Both plates contained a golden-brown grilled turkey and cheese cut diagonally into triangles. "Got any idea which cupboard has the coffee mugs?" he asked, turning back to the refrigerator.

"Uh uh," Jerry mumbled around a mouthful of chip and dip while Leo pulled the milk out and set it down.

"I'll find 'em," Leo replied confidently. He did on his third try, grabbing a pair of them. He placed them on the counter before he opened the milk, then he began pouring it into the mugs. "Are you lactose intolerant or allergic to anything?"

Leo didn't want to make his mate sick.

"No, and nothing that I'm aware of." Jerry's brows furrowed as he cocked his head. "Although, I can't think of ever eating anything exotic over the years. The staples at home were all basic, and then when I was on the streets, I ate whatever I could get my hands on. Then after when—" He paused, his cheeks flushing pink.

Nodding, Leo didn't need Jerry to finish. He got it. With how slender Jerry's frame was, he would bet his left nut that the asshole gangsters didn't feed him well.

"Here. Enjoy," Leo encouraged, placing the mug before Jerry. He left the milk out in case they needed more and took a seat beside Jerry. "I like to dip my *Oreos*. Makes 'em a little mushy."

Jerry was too busy shoving a corner of sandwich into his mouth to respond. After he bit off a bite and began to chew, he nodded. His expression seemed to be one of longing as he eyed the still-sealed bag of cookies.

After Leo grabbed a wedge of his own sandwich and took a big bite, he put it down and wiped his fingers on a napkin. He chewed slowly, enjoying the cheesy, crunchy goodness, and reached for the bag of cookies. Easing his forefingers under the tab and gripping the top with his thumb, Leo pulled the re-sealable flap back, then rolled it carefully so the stickiness caught on the edge and held itself open.

Leo swallowed while grabbing a cookie. With a wink at Jerry, he dipped his cookie into the milk. He lifted it, allowing it to drip into the cup a few times, before popping it into his mouth.

To Leo's relief, Jerry followed his example. The hum of appreciation that rumbled from the human caused Leo's prick to twitch behind his fly. His smile of appreciation, however, that warmed something deep in Leo's chest.

Eating in companionable silence, Leo made it through his sandwich, ate another cookie, then enjoyed a number of chips, skimming them through the French onion dip each time. As he ate another cookie, Leo noticed Jerry glancing between his last sandwich triangle and the cookie package. He was nibbling on his bottom lip, his expression betraying his indecision.

"What's up?" Leo asked curiously. Reaching out—it was so damn hard not to touch with his mate sitting right next to him—Leo teased the backs of his fingertips down the soft flesh of Jerry's upper arm. "Something wrong?"

Jerry started, his head whipping around so he could peer at Leo. His mouth opened, closed, then he stated, "I'm getting full, and I really want another cookie." He glanced at his sandwich. "But I don't want to waste it."

Realizing Jerry's dilemma, Leo grinned. "Have a cookie," he urged, reaching over and grabbing the sandwich from his mate's plate. When Jerry met his gaze once more, Leo winked and added, "Or two or three," before biting the triangle in half.

Barking a laugh, Jerry returned his grin. His face lit up as he reached for the cookie package, took two, and put them on his plate. Holding one, he dipped it in his milk.

Leo smiled as he finished the sandwich. While he hadn't been hungry when he'd arrived, as a shifter, he could eat just about any time. Serving food to his mate also helped settle his wolf, since Leo guessed it would be a while before he could connect with him physically.

While Jerry was finishing the second cookie he'd taken, Leo's sensitive hearing picked up the sound of approaching footsteps. He realized his time alone with his mate was nearing an end. Pushing down his disappointment, Leo downed the last of his slightly chocolaty milk before turning on his barstool to face the door.

Leo knew his movement would alert Jerry of the approaching visitors, too. That way his human wouldn't be startled again. Leo had hated the fear-filled, deer-in-the-headlights look Jerry had sported when he'd first walked in on him.

As Leo watched the dining room door open, Jerry was wiping his fingers on a napkin. Smiling at who entered, Leo dipped his head as he greeted, "Alpha Declan."

"Leo, glad ye could make it." The big, African American's Irish accent was a bit deeper than normal, betraying his fatigue . . . as did the lines etched around his eyes and mouth. "Have ye filled Jerry in on why ye're here?"

"Uh, no, Alpha," Leo admitted, his cheeks heating a little. "Got distracted with food." He waved toward their mini spread.

"Food is good." Alpha Declan rounded the bar and grabbed a mug from the cupboard. "Looks yummy," he added, picking up the milk and pouring it into his mug. Then he lifted the jug toward their cups while lifting a brow in silent question, obviously asking if they wanted more. After they'd both shaken their heads, Declan put it back in the fridge. "Now's a good time, then," he stated as he grabbed a cookie. Before biting it in half, he tipped his chin toward Leo and stated, "Why don't you share with Jerry your job, Leo?"

Leo mentally winced as Jerry turned his worry-filled gaze toward him. "Relax, Jer. It's nothing bad." Resting his left elbow on the counter, he leaned forward just a little as he returned his mate's regard with what he hoped was a reassuring smile. "I was asked to come here because, in our shifter pack, we have a problem unique to paranormals. We're pretty long-lived, often upward toward five hundred years." Seeing Jerry's eyes widen, Leo was pleased that his scent registered surprise as opposed to fear or concern. That was good, right? "Because paranormals hide in plain sight, we have to create a new identity for ourselves every few decades, or the humans we know will get suspicious of why we don't age."

Leo watched Jerry's lips part into an *oh* as he nodded, although he wasn't certain exactly how much his mate actually comprehended. "So, what I do for my pack-mates is create new identities." He waggled his brows as he leaned even closer. "We'll spend time together, explore your interests a bit, and figure out where you want to go from here." Seeing Jerry's eyes widen and his head tip, his expression betraying his racing thoughts, Leo reached over and gripped his arm, just above his elbow, squeezing lightly. "You don't have to make a decision right now, sweetheart."

Gods, I hope I don't spook him with the endearments.

Leo knew it wasn't the first time he'd called Jerry something like that, but he couldn't seem to help himself. They just kept rolling off his tongue. It was just so damn natural.

The feel of Jerry's light muscling over soft flesh caused goose bumps to erupt on his own arm. His palm warmed, and he barely resisted his urge to slide his hand up under the short sleeve of Jerry's t-shirt. When his mate glanced at where Leo held him, his brows furrowing, he forced himself to release him . . . after giving him one more light squeeze.

"I-I don't know," Jerry mumbled, turning his attention to his empty plate.

"Like I said," Leo replied. "No rush. We have all the time in the world for us to explore different activities and figure out your likes and dislikes."

And during that time, Leo had every intention of figuring out how to woo his mate.

Jerry glanced between Leo and Declan. His expression turned wary, and his eyes narrowed. "Why are you doing this?" He frowned. "What's it cost?"

"Nothing," Alpha Declan immediately replied. "It won't cost ye anything." It was obvious Jerry didn't believe them, and the alpha sighed as he grabbed another cookie. Waving it in the air almost absently, Declan explained, shrugging. "Consider yourself collateral damage to our raid. While we were kicking ass and taking names, you had your world expanded. That makes ye our responsibility."

Then Declan popped the cookie into his mouth.

"I-I'm your, uh . . . your obligation then?" From the sound of his voice, Jerry didn't seem too pleased by that revelation.

"Hey." Leo's need to soothe drove out common sense. Sliding to the edge of his seat, he rested his left hand on Jerry's thigh. Massaging the thin, muscular leg beneath his palm, Leo held Jerry's wide-eyed gaze. "I'm not sure what thought just popped into your head, but we don't consider this a bad thing."

Jerry scowled at him, scoffing derisively. "Sure. If I hadn't seen your cousin turn into a wolf and tear Linds apart, I would've been shunted off to the police with the rest of the gang's whores." Curling his lip, he crossed his arms over his chest. "Let me assure you. Right now, the rest of them aren't in this cushy mansion"—he uncoiled an arm and waved around the space absently—"being offered a new identity."

"Ask what ye really mean, Jerry," Declan urged quietly, appearing interested and not in the least upset. "Nothing ye say here will cause ill will between us."

"Why didn't you help all of us?" Jerry cried, slamming his fists on his counter. Just as swiftly, he crumpled in on himself, wrapping his arms around his torso. "I'm not anything special. Some of the guys there . . . they were new. They could have used a second chance so much more than me. I . . . I'm damaged goods. I'm not worth anything anymore. I—"

Unable to bear listening to Jerry denigrate himself anymore, Leo growled softly. He squeezed his human's thigh lightly. When Jerry whipped his head up and focused on him, Leo shook his head.

"That's enough, Jerry," Leo growled roughly. Seeing Jerry's eyes widen and his face pale, he sucked in a harsh breath as he bit back another snarl attempting to escape him.

Once he thought he had control of himself, Leo moved his hand from Jerry's thigh, lifting it slowly, lightly cradling his mate's jaw. Leo couldn't begin to express how pleased he felt that his human didn't flinch from him. "You were led to us by Fate, sweetheart. Already I feel blessed to have met you." While Leo knew his mate didn't understand, he had to continue with, "My life would have been poorer for it if I hadn't."

Jerry's brows furrowed, and his lips pinched, but it was no longer in anger or frustration. Instead, he just seemed confused. "Why?" Jerry whispered. "Why would you say something like that?"

"Because it's the truth," Leo replied. Hopefully soon, he would have the opportunity to explain it all, too, but he knew now wasn't yet the time. No way was Jerry ready for Leo to share that he was the other half of his soul. Instead, Leo told him, "And you are more than worthy of another chance, sweetheart. Now." Leo smiled as he stroked his thumb along Jerry's jawline. "Tell me you believe me."

It took a second, but finally, Jerry whispered, "I believe you."

"Good." Leo began to dip his head, wanting to taste Jerry's trembling lips.

It was probably good that Alpha Declan took that second to interrupt. Jerry wasn't really ready.

"And in the meantime, I'll work with Detective Malone to guarantee that your fellow captives will all be assured new lives, too."

"You'll do that?" Jerry murmured, turning and gaping at the alpha, pulling from Leo's hold. "Why?" Just as he finished the question, a deep yawn took him.

Alpha Declan chuckled softly. "Because you're right. You *all* deserve a second chance after what ye endured." He pushed away from the counter, grabbing the cookie package and re-sealing it in the process. "Head to bed, Jerry. You've had a long day, and ye must be exhausted." Smiling warmly, he added, "Besides, I need a word with Leo here before I send him up to check on his family."

Even though Leo didn't want to let his mate go, he did it, watching Jerry shuffle out of the dining room before returning his focus to Alpha Declan.

His alpha smirked, his deep gray eyes radiating warmth. "Congratulations."

Leo grinned broadly. "Thanks."

Chapter Four

With a squeak, Jerry jolted back to wakefulness. He glanced around wildly for a few seconds, taking in the lavish surroundings. His heart pounded, and his breathing caught in his chest.

Recalling the previous evening, Jerry let out a heavy sigh and closed his eyes. He settled back in the nest of blankets he'd made on the padded window seat. While the bed had been inviting, after being so long in a windowless room, the allure of staring outside had been too much to resist.

Heck-fire, if I could have, I would have slept on the balcony.

Too bad it was way too cold for that.

For the first time in . . . almost six years, he was free.

Jerry wasn't even certain what that meant anymore. With his forehead resting against the cool glass, he peered out the window. When he'd been young, he'd had so many hopes and dreams. Now . . . he couldn't think of one.

Jerry took in the way the morning sun illuminated the horizon and smiled. He couldn't remember the last time he'd watched a sunrise. Even though he'd only managed to sleep for a few hours, Jerry couldn't resist seeing more.

Wanting to be a part of that, Jerry eased out from under the blankets and stood. Grabbing the comforter, he wrapped it around his shoulders, then padded to the door. Jerry paused just long enough to grab his battered sneakers where he'd left them beside the door and to be certain he didn't hear any movement in the hall outside before easing from the room.

As Jerry made his way downstairs, he recalled how he hadn't heard the arrival of Leo and Manon the evening before. He figured the house was just too big to confirm that no one else was up.

Jerry still felt relief when he made it to the back foyer without meeting anyone. It wasn't that he was anti-social. He just didn't know how to interact with people anymore . . . especially since these men knew exactly what he was.

After sliding his feet into his shoes, Jerry headed outside. He kept the blanket pulled tight around his shoulders with one hand on the inside. With his other hand, he bundled up the excess blanket, holding it off the ground.

The chilly, early morning air almost felt like a slap in the face, but Jerry welcomed it. He found himself smiling as he strode swiftly across the massive back patio with the empty stone fire pit. Making his way into a dormant garden, he found a stone bench near a large fountain . . . which was still functioning.

Jerry settled on the bench, bundling several layers of the blanket under his butt to insulate himself against the cold. Tucking his legs under the bench, he tipped his head back and allowed his eyelids to slide closed. He inhaled deeply, relishing the fresh, morning air as he enjoyed the sounds of the trickling fountain.

Unwilling to miss the sunrise, Jerry opened his eyes and focused on the horizon. He smiled vacantly as first the sky turned gray, then lightened to blue. Finally, the vibrant yellow of the sun peeked over the horizon, burning up the morning mist and forcing Jerry to avert his gaze.

The trickle of the fountain combined with the sounds of morning birds twittering in the trees began to lull Jerry's mind. His eyelids slid closed. He swayed a little on the bench, sighing. It would be so tempting to curl up on the bench. With the warmth of the sun on his face, he could drift right off and—

"Well, well, well." A snide tenor voice cut through Jerry's relaxed thoughts. "Looks like this gang is a little lax in keeping an eye on their possessions."

Snapping open his eyes, Jerry tensed as he whipped his head around. He gasped when he spotted five men slinking from between garden bushes, being led by a smirking dirty-blond-haired man. That man exchanged glances with the pair on either side of him.

Jerry recognized the looks on that pair—greed, lust, and smugness. A quick glance at the final two men told Jerry that they were busy looking around, obviously keeping an eye on the area. When Jerry returned his focus to the speaker, recognition finally hit.

"Myron Sandserson," Jerry hissed.

Tension thrummed through him as he watched Myron's lips curl into a sneer. "You don't have the right to say my name, whore." Snapping his fingers, he pointed at his feet. "Kneel." As if expecting him to obey without question, Myron turned his attention to the men on his left. "Sanchez, go with Burman and see if any of the other whores these guys took from the Robles gang are just wandering around." His expression turned cruel as he added, "Whores that are already mostly trained will start the money rolling in faster than having to teach new merchandise their place." His eyes narrowed as he snickered nastily. "No way are we letting some new gang take Robles territory that should have been our's anyway." As the pair of men disappeared amidst the dormant bushes, Myron returned his focus to Jerry. "Why haven't you moved, yet, whore?"

Jerry sat frozen, unable to make himself move. He wanted to leap up and run, to scream and call for help. But his body wouldn't obey.

When Jerry saw Myron reach for him, he finally jerked himself out of his stupor. With a squeak, he leaped away from the man. Releasing the blanket, he nearly tripped over it as he lunged to the right and began sprinting back toward the house.

Unfortunately, Jerry still couldn't get his voice to work. His heart hammering in his throat seemed to stop up his voice box. Hearing someone's heavy footfalls pounding behind him didn't help matters. Jerry didn't know if it was Myron or one of his other goons, and he was too terrified of tripping to chance glancing over his shoulder.

Movement to his right caused Jerry to shy to the left. He heard the thud of a body hitting the ground just as arms wrapped around his torso. Finally, he found his voice.

Jerry's high-pitched scream rent the air.

"Easy, sweetheart. Easy, Jer. You're okay. You're safe. Hush, baby."

Leo's deep crooning voice registered in Jerry's terrified brain at about the same time as the big man's earthy scent registered in his nose. Finding both soothing, Jerry sagged against the man. He turned in Leo's embrace and gripped his t-shirt with both hands as he buried his face against Leo's torso.

"That's it. You're safe," Leo continued to whisper. He kept one hand wrapped securely around Jerry's waist, holding him close. Using his other hand, he rubbed up and down Jerry's spine. "No one will ever harm you again. You have my word."

Realizing he couldn't bury his head in the sand, so to speak—not if Leo was to have a chance at keeping his promise—Jerry lifted his head. "There's more of them," he whispered, his voice a little hoarse and scratchy from his screaming.

Jerry glanced to his right and spotted the unconscious

figure of one of Myron's right-hand men. Luther stood over him, his hands clenching and unclenching as if struggling with something . . . maybe a desire to snap the guy's neck. Jerry sure appreciated that the dark expression wasn't aimed at him.

"Myron is back that way with a guard," Jerry told the cousins, untangling the fingers of his right hand from Leo's shirt so he could point. "And there's two more on the grounds s-searching f-for more wh-wh-whores."

"They won't find any here," Leo stated on a growl. Lifting his hand, he cupped Jerry's jaw and forced him to tip his head up and meet his gaze. "Wanna know why?"

Furrowing his brows, Jerry tried to understand the glitter in Leo's eyes and the firm slant of his lips. "Why?"

"Because there are no whores here, Jerry," Leo stated, his voice quiet and firm. "None at all."

Jerry opened his mouth, but no sound came out. He snapped his mouth shut so he could swallow hard. He didn't understand how Leo could believe that, but from the firm expression on his face, he sure seemed to.

Uncertain what the right thing to say was, Jerry simply nodded.

"Come on," Luther urged softly, his voice holding a gruff quality. "Let's take this asshole back to his friends. I'm sure the others have rounded them up by now."

That caught Jerry's attention. He tore his focus from Leo's handsome face and turned to peer at Luther. The man was almost as big as Leo but nowhere near as good looking. At least, Jerry thought so.

Leo nodded, releasing Jerry only long enough to turn him before returning his arm around his waist.

Unable to resist the offered comfort, Jerry snuggled against Leo's side as they began heading back the way he'd just come. He watched as Luther lifted the fallen gangbanger and tossed him over his shoulder. Luther made it look easy, reminding Jerry that the people around him weren't human.

Suddenly, Jerry thought he was okay with that. Being held against Leo, even though they were headed back toward the second-in-command of the Domingo gang, he still felt safe. He found it to be a novel experience as it had been so very rare over the last half dozen years.

The sound of voices reached Jerry before he spotted the men.

"You know, I had intended to leave your gang alone, since your gang didn't traffic in humans." The melodious tenor sounded mildly bored. "But seeing as you've decided the fill the gap created by the downfall of the Robles gang—" A cold chuckle filled the air. "Now, it will be my genuine pleasure to destroy you all."

"You better be careful what you say to me, gringo." Jerry recognized Myron's voice. "You won't like what will happen if I think I'm threatened."

Jerry and his group rounded the bend, revealing Myron standing in the path where he'd left him. The difference was the gun that had been tucked into the waistband of his jeans was no longer there. The guard who'd stayed with him had also been unarmed, and he now knelt on the cold ground.

The other pair were still nowhere to be seen.

Peering at the men that Myron glared maliciously at, Jerry tried to remember their names. He recognized Declan, of course. The huge African American sat on the bench Jerry had vacated, and he stared at Myron with a cold expression.

A broad-shouldered Native American stood nearby. He was one half of the vocal pair he'd heard the previous evening. Jerry was pretty sure his name started with a C, but he couldn't place it. Next to him was his much smaller lover. He had light-brown hair, hazel eyes, and a wiry frame. That man held some kind of handgun in his right hand and tapped it almost absently against his thigh.

"Ah, you brought my merchandise back to me. I suppose that will make up for what your guy did to my man there," Myron stated, glancing at Jerry and the guy Luther unceremoniously dropped on the ground. Myron's eyes narrowed, "If he's permanently injured, I'm—"

Quick as a striking snake, the small man lashed out. He slammed his gun across Myron's face, causing the big gangster to stumble backward and drop to one knee. Myron's glare was filled with hatred as he lifted his left hand to his mouth and wiped blood from his split lip.

"You're gonna pay for that, gringo," Myron snarled.

Just as Myron finished speaking, the sound of approaching footsteps drew everyone's attention. From around a bend in a path appeared the two other gangsters. Jerry's heartrate spiked for a second, but then he spotted Manon and a redheaded woman behind them, each of them carrying a gun and pointing it at the strangers.

The sneer on Myron's lips remained, but his face paled a little.

"Now that we're all here," began the guy who'd just pistol-whipped Myron. "Allow me to make introductions." He pointed at himself, then at a few others. "I'm Jared. This is my lover, Carson. That's our boss-man, Declan." He pointed at Jerry. "That nice man you tried to kidnap is Jerry. He's not merchandise, and neither are any other humans around here."

"You're faggots?" Myron blurted out, derision in his voice.

Jared offered a wide smile that looked more creepy than happy. "You just keep digging a deeper hole, Myron." While Myron's eyes opened just a little wider, betraying his surprise, Jared laughed. "Yep, I know who you are."

"Then you should know that your only option is letting

me go." Myron rose back to his feet, his expression gaining confidence. "Otherwise" — he waved his hand, indicating the house and grounds—"all this will be gone within a day."

"You seem to be under the impression that anything you say matters to me." Jared smirked at Myron, appearing more than a little amused. "It doesn't." His lips parted in a wide grin. "In fact, you will just be the first."

Without preamble, Jared lifted his gun and pointed it at Myron's chest. The gangster must have finally recognized his mistake, for his eyes widened, and he opened his mouth—maybe to beg for mercy. Myron didn't get the chance. Two shots in rapid succession echoed through the morning air.

Myron's body toppled, blood blooming on its torso.

Jerry gasped, staring as shock filled him.

Leo tightened the arm around Jerry's waist. At the same time, he placed his palm along his temple. He used the hold to turn Jerry's face toward his chest, pressing his head into him.

Closing his eyes, Jerry fought against the trembles that suddenly began racking his body. He'd seen plenty of men killed over the years, so he wasn't totally certain what he was feeling. Instead of trying to parse out the sensations, he focused on the men shouting just out of his line of sight, but he didn't turn to look at anyone.

"Now, gentlemen," Jared stated, sounding bored. "You can either tell me what I want to know, or you can join Myron."

"Go to hell!" one guy cried.

That was followed by a couple more shots, and Jared replied glibly, "After you."

Jerry couldn't help it. A hysterical giggle escaped him.

"Easy, Jerry," Leo murmured into his ear. "They'll never hurt you again."

Nodding, Jerry lifted his head. "That's not it," he mumbled, his heart tripping wildly in his chest. "I should feel bad, yet . . . all I feel is—" Jerry paused, shaking his head.

To Jerry's relief, Leo's smile held a wealth of understanding. "Vindication? Satisfaction? Maybe even a little pleasure and relief?"

Jerry nodded as he nibbled his bottom lip.

Luther stepped close and rumbled, "That's totally normal. People like these assholes hurt you for years." Crossing his arms over his chest, he added, "They deserve everything Jared is going to give them and more." A cold smile curved his lips. "And don't you worry. It'll happen, too."

"What do you mean?" Jerry heard the sound of a gun again, and it occurred to him that the cousins were leading him away from the action. That was just fine with him. "What's going to happen?"

Leo grinned down at him. "Alpha Declan has given Jared free rein in this case."

Luther chuckled once more. "That means Jared is going to clean house . . . literally."

"And he likes to blow things up," Leo added, snorting. "And while he does that, we're going to take you some place safe."

"Where?" If the estate with all the fences and security wasn't safe, where would be?

"There's a cabin we own back home in the mountains of Colorado, and recently, the renters moved out. We're going there," Leo told him. He paused and turned Jerry to look at him, keeping one hand on his waist and using the other to cup his jaw and tilt his chin up. "That way you can take your time deciding what you want to do in a safe environment." After a second, Leo's expression turned uncertain as he asked, "Is that okay?"

Jerry hesitated an instant. Alone in a secluded place with

Leo? Even as he wondered how he would manage to hide his attraction to the man, he nodded and found himself saying, "Yes."

Seeing Leo's pleased grin caused Jerry's heart to trip in his chest.

I might be in trouble for a whole new reason.

He sure liked seeing Leo happy, though.

CHAPTER FIVE

Leo figured he'd railroaded Jerry into coming with him and his family back to Stone Ridge, seeing as he'd asked his mate at a vulnerable moment. Still, now that he had his human back in shifter territory, his wolf felt so much happier. Leo's animal wasn't a very patient creature, and he didn't understand why they couldn't seduce and claim their pretty human immediately.

It wasn't often Leo found himself at odds with his wolf, and it left him a bit unsettled. Still, for his mate, he would deal with it. Leo would give Jerry as much time as he needed.

"Wow," Jerry whispered, glancing around with interest. "This place is . . . you called it a cabin, but it really looks like a farmhouse?" As he finished speaking, his brows drew together, a shadow crossing over his features. After swallowing hard enough to cause his Adam's apple to bob, Jerry whispered, "And look at all this snow!"

Leo peered through the windshield of his pick-up truck. Taking in the large structure, he winced. While he and his family had always referred to it as the family cabin, it did look like a farmhouse.

His father had given the structure a facelift and expansion around eighty years before . . . when he'd put in indoor plumbing. Before the renovation, it had been a two-bedroom, off-the-grid cabin with an outhouse. Once Leo's dad had finished, the place boasted seven bedrooms, four bathrooms, and two fireplaces—one in the great room and one in the master bedroom at the back of the house. When both fireplaces were roaring, they would heat the entire home, even in the winter time.

Wanting to ease whatever had caused Jerry's concern, Leo decided to tell him all about it. He exited the cab, then reached back in and grabbed his duffle bag from behind the seat. As he did that, he started to talk.

Leo led the way through the foot-high snow, using his legs to create trenches for Jerry to follow in. He told about his great grandfather and how he'd built the first cabin. While unlocking the door and guiding his mate inside, he explained how their family had used the cabin as a getaway from the rising human population. They'd also coordinated family pack runs from there, too.

When Alpha Declan had moved his pack to the area, Leo's grandfather had moved on. That had been over a hundred years before. When Leo's father had chosen to stay, it had split the family—some leaving and some staying. Leo and most of Leo's father's side had stuck around. Luther was his father's sister's son, and most of that side had left.

Leo and Luther had always been best friends, and his buddy had chosen to stay . . . the last remnant of that side of the family. That was what made him so close to his cousin, so instead of thinking of Stephani as a second cousin, she immediately became an honorary cousin. Hell, since the girl's mother had never been in the picture, they'd practically raised her together.

While Leo and Jerry trooped from his truck to the house, he explained all those things. The time it took to make several trips gave him plenty of time. They gathered all Jerry's newly purchased clothes—jeans, t-shirts, flannel shirts, thick socks, and a heavy coat, not to mention a pair of hiking boots as well as a pair of snow boots. Leo had loved providing for his mate. On top of that, they'd had to carry in all the groceries. Due to the sometimes unpredictable weather in the mountains, Leo had made certain they had enough food for several weeks.

That included the fact that Luther, Deke, and Stephani would be joining them in a few days or so. Leo also guessed that, within the week, he would see Sara—Declan's daughter, who'd also been rescued—and her human mate, Ricky. The detective still hadn't—at least as far as Leo had heard—accepted that he was a shifter's mate, even though he'd known about paranormals for a few years.

Leo couldn't imagine how that made Sara feel.

By the time they'd brought everything in, Jerry shivered in his new coat. He seemed far more relaxed about their location, at least. Whatever had been bothering him appeared to have passed the more Leo talked.

Good.

Settling Jerry on the bearskin rug before the fireplace, Leo set about building a roaring blaze. It only took him a moment to lay the logs. Then he used old newspaper that had been left in a magazine rack to light it. Once he had the flames caught, he headed to the sofa and grabbed a throw blanket off the back of it.

Leo knelt behind Jerry and wrapped the blanket around his human's shoulders. Taking advantage of the moment, he rubbed his hands over his shoulders and down his upper arms. Even through the thick fabric of blanket and coat, Leo could feel his mate's slender limbs and thin shoulders.

My sweet human needs a bit of weight.

Dipping his head, Leo pressed a kiss to the side of Jerry's neck. He hesitated there, inhaling deeply. His mouth watered, and his blood heated, swiftly flowing south.

Less than a day and a half in Jerry's company, most of it spent traveling and shopping, and Leo was already having a tough time controlling himself.

"Are you smelling me?" Jerry whispered suddenly, turning his head just enough to meet Leo's gaze out of the corner of his eye.

Leo knew he was busted but decided that wasn't such a bad thing. They needed to talk about it sometime. Holding Jerry's gaze, he nuzzled his nose against his cheek for a second before inhaling deeply.

Finally, Leo lifted his head enough to reveal his smile. "Yeah, Jer," he admitted. "You smell good to me, to my wolf." Turning his head, Leo pressed a light kiss to Jerry's cheek. "It's rare to find a scent as heady as yours." Seeing the way Jerry's brows furrowed just a smidge and how he nibbled his bottom lip, Leo asked, "Does it bother you?"

"I saw the way Declan and Luther would smell their, uh, partners," Jerry murmured, his expression turning confused. "It means something. Doesn't it?"

Leo couldn't—and would never—lie to his mate. He nodded. "Yeah, sweetheart," he murmured, doing his best to keep his smile relaxed and confident. "Paranormals have something called a mate." He hesitated, trying to decide on the best way to explain. Noticing the way the furrow between Jerry's brows deepened, Leo decided to say, "A paranormal longs to find their mate, the other half of their soul. Their mate is their perfect complement. Someone who can complete them."

When Leo spotted how Jerry's eyes widened and his entire body stiffened, he remembered how he'd soothed that reaction earlier—by talking, explaining. Taking heed of that learning experience, Leo bussed a kiss to his mate's lips, then straightened even as he settled on the floor. Leo wrapped his arms around Jerry's shoulders, urging his human to lean back against him.

As Leo did that, he shared, "I would have been attracted to you anyway, Jerry." He could feel the tension thrumming through his mate's body, so he did his best to keep his tone soft and reassuring. "Just like I know you're attracted to me. Being mates, that just happened to make what we're feeling more intense. Our connection means"—Leo hesitated an instant, then admitted—"if you give us a chance, we'll come to care about each other, understand each other, and soon enough, love each other, very quickly."

For what felt like a long moment, Jerry didn't respond. Leo had to remind himself to keep breathing. Staring into the fire, watching the flames lick at the burning pieces, he did his best to be patient . . . to wait for his mate to process what he'd shared.

"Why would you want someone like me?" Jerry finally whispered. "My own family didn't want me because of"—a shudder went through him—"what I am." As soon as the words were out of Jerry's mouth, he hunched forward, curling in on himself.

"What you are?" Leo repeated slowly, recalling his research. "Because you're gay? Is that why you ended up on the streets, Jerry?"

Jerry nodded his head where he rested it on his knees. With his arms around his shins, he was obviously making himself the smallest target possible. The move also did a decent job of protecting his soft spots . . . as if he were waiting for a punch or kick.

Leo hated what the nonverbal information was telling him. His mate had had a damn tough life.

Not anymore though.

"Do you think less of Alpha Declan and his doctor mate? Or Stephani? Or Luther and his partner, Deke?" Leo murmured the questions into Jerry's ear, hoping his quiet tones would help to soothe him. When several minutes passed without Jerry responding, he pressed, "Do you think less of me because I consider myself bisexual? Or maybe you think I'm not good enough for you because I've slept with so many people that I've lost count."

Finally, that got a response.

Jerry turned his head, meeting Leo's gaze, and gaped at him.

At least he's no longer curled up.

Leo shrugged one shoulder, twisting his lips into a wry smile. "It's true," he admitted. "I'm about a decade shy of two hundred years old, Jer. That's a long time to be having sex." Gliding his left hand up Jerry's blanket-covered chest, Leo cradled his jaw. He rubbed his thumb along Jerry's bottom lip lightly, enjoying the plump flesh he wanted to nibble, tease, and taste. "On the other hand, that means I'll be damn good at pleasing you."

"Y-You're worried I won't want you?" Jerry responded incredulously. "That's ridiculous." Then he paused, cocking his head.

Just smiling back at him, Leo waited, hoping his mate would share whatever had popped into his head.

"So, um, those other guys. They're mates. Does that mean they're lovers, too? They're all, um . . . gay?" Jerry whispered the last word, as if it were dirty or something.

Leo figured that had been trained into him — probably first by his parents and their church, then by the gangs that had essentially owned him. He figured he had his work cut out for himself to change that idea. Years of programming wouldn't be changed overnight.

"Yes, Jerry," Leo answered, keeping his voice warm. It was tough because all he wanted to do was track down every asshole that had hurt Jerry and destroy them. "Alpha Declan and Doctor Lark Trystan are mates and partners in all ways. Same as the others you saw there. Manon's partner is waiting at home for him to return." Leo offered a reassuring smile as he continued, "I know you've been told your entire life that what you feel is wrong, but it's just not true, my mate."

Leo slid his hand up into Jerry's thick red hair and cradled his skull. "What we feel for each other. It's totally natural." Seeing the flare of hope light up his mate's eyes, Leo hoped he was getting through. He also knew he needed to be honest and straightforward. Jerry deserved nothing less. "I long to be able to explore everything we could have together. Now that I've met you, you're the most important person in my life."

"Is being mates like, well, marriage?"

"You're so smart." Leo couldn't help but grin at how swiftly Jerry was putting everything together. "Yes, Jer. Mating is like marriage . . . but more. Once we bond, there's no such thing as divorce." Unable to hide his growl just at the thought of his mate wanting to leave him, Leo added, "Shifters don't cheat, and if another were to touch you, I would kill them." He saw the way Jerry's eyes widened, so he quickly racked his brain for the good points. "I'll always strive to keep you happy. Your health and safety will always be my goals. And sated." His blood heated just at the thought. "I wish to show you all the pleasure your body can experience at my touch."

"Y-You'd pleasure me?" Jerry's lips parted, and his breath came in soft pants. "Really?"

"Absolutely," Leo replied, his own arousal spiking at the growing scent of Jerry's arousal. His human definitely liked that idea. "I will give you so much bliss that you pass out from it. That will be my goal."

Jerry scoffed as he rolled his eyes. "That's not possible."

Leo grinned broadly. "Are you challenging me?" He chuckled huskily. "I do like the sound of that." Then he sobered. "But once we begin, there is no turning back." Sliding the hand he had in Jerry's hair down to his nape, Leo tightened his right arm, pulling him flush to his chest. "I would like nothing more than to suck your cock until you spill in my mouth, so I can drink your seed."

From the way Jerry's breath hitched, and how his eyes widened, Leo knew his mate liked that idea, too.

"It will start the bonding process, though, Jerry," Leo warned. Sliding his palm under the blanket, Leo ran into his mate's thick coat. *Right. At least, I've warmed him up.* "Shall I give you time to think about it?"

Leo couldn't resist adding just a bit of persuasion. *So much for being patient.* He eased his hand downward some more, finding Jerry's fly and cupping the bulge. Pressing and massaging lightly, Leo dipped his head and nipped at the side of Jerry's neck.

"Think about what you want, my mate," Leo rumbled gruffly. "I'm not a patient man, but I'll do the best I can with you. Tell me the pace you want to go."

Jerry groaned and shuddered in his hold. "That makes it sound like I don't truly have a choice."

Leo released Jerry's groin and moved his palm to his thigh. Lifting his head, he held his mate's heavy-lidded gaze. "That's a true statement, Jerry," he stated. For good or ill, he answered honestly. "The second I scented you, there was no going back for either of us."

With bated breath, Leo waited for Jerry's response.

Chapter Six

Holy camoles!

Jerry couldn't ever remember being so turned on.

And Leo expects me to think?

While Jerry figured he was staying quiet for too long, he couldn't seem to find his tongue. Really, how was he supposed to pull any thoughts together with his dick throbbing so badly? He'd almost moaned when Leo had removed his hand. While he'd occasionally gotten off when a john fucked him, which had always left him feeling even dirtier than when he didn't get off, Jerry had never *ever* been hard before the process started.

Now he was thinking about begging to be fucked.

How is this possible?

Just as quickly, Jerry knew the answer was simple. Paranormals were real. Shifters were real. That meant magick and mates and bonds were real, too.

When Leo rose to his feet and moved toward the fire, an intense sensation coursed through Jerry. It took him a couple of heartbeats to recognize it. As he watched Leo add a couple more logs to the fire, Jerry realized he felt . . . bereft.

Jerry had only felt it once before, when he'd been kicked out by his family, and he had hated the feeling then, too.

"Cock tease," Jerry blurted out, his confusion and frustration finally allowing him to find his tongue. The next second, embarrassment flooded him. He couldn't believe he'd said that.

Leo spun around where he crouched and pinned him

with a look that appeared almost . . . feral.

Sucking in a swift breath, Jerry felt his cheeks blaze, and he knew he blushed. Unable to hold Leo's hungry gaze, he lowered his chin. The need to watch out for the big man's response was too ingrained in Jerry, so he peered at him from beneath his lashes.

Except, Leo didn't swing a hand to smack him upside the head or across the mouth. Instead, he eased onto his hands and knees and crawled across the couple of steps between them. Leo pushed his nose against Jerry's neck and inhaled, openly scenting him.

The hairs on Jerry's neck stood on end, and goose bumps broke out on his shoulders. Tingles erupted through his torso, and his breath caught in his throat. When the sensation hit his groin, Jerry whimpered.

"Gods, Jer," Leo rumbled, nuzzling his skin. "That's a beautiful sound."

Leo nipped Jerry's neck where it met his shoulder, creating a fresh wash of zings that caused Jerry's nipples to bead.

"And I'm not a cock tease, sweetheart," Leo countered gruffly. "If you say the word, I will oh-so-happily take care of you."

Then Leo sucked on Jerry's pulse point, ruining any chance of finding his tongue that he had. Each pull at his neck caused his dick to twitch. Feeling pre-cum ooze from his erection, Jerry moaned. He released the blanket and rested his palms on the rug behind him, needing to lock his elbows in order to stay upright.

With just those few touches, Leo was reducing his body to *Jello*.

"Gods, baby," Leo muttered on a groan. "You look so gorgeous lost in lust like this." He nuzzled his cheek along Jerry's neck, his five o' clock shadow rasping lightly against his skin. "But I need you to tell me what you want, my mate.

If you don't want this, I need to pull away, or I won't be able to stop." Leo rumbled a gruff growl before finishing, "You just smell and respond so damn good. I want you so fucking badly."

Jerry whimpered. He knew his mind was a mess. How could it not be? With his body on fire, Jerry's brain was in no condition to make a decision, but he knew he had to.

Deciding to focus on something non-sexual, Jerry latched onto a memory. "Y-You said that, um—" Closing his eyes, he breathed through his nose in an effort to draw his thoughts together. When Leo stopped kissing and sucking on his neck, putting a bit of space between his mouth and Jerry's skin, he felt a mixture of relief and disappointment. At least the move allowed him the opportunity to think. "You said that we would spend time figuring out, um, what I like?" Jerry turned his head so he could meet Leo's gaze fully. "Is that still something we're doing? Even way out here?"

The hunger eased from Leo's expression just a smidge, and his lips curved into a wide smile. "Oh, yes, Jer," he assured, nodding once. "Yes, we'll definitely be exploring your likes and dislikes." Waggling his brows, Leo added, "I can't know how to please you if I don't know what you like or don't like, right?"

Jerry felt a light, crazy buoyant sensation that he couldn't recall experiencing in . . . forever.

Hope.

Returning Leo's grin, Jerry nodded. He rocked forward and wrapped his arms around the bigger man's neck. His momentum reversed, and he began tumbling back to the rug.

While Leo probably could have stopped them, the bigger man went with it. Levering over Jerry, Leo smiled down at him. He caught his weight on his forearms, which he rested on either side of Jerry's head.

"So, my mate," Leo murmured, his hazel eyes full of warmth as he peered at him. "What do you think?"

"I think," Jerry began, licking his lips as he lowered his focus from Leo's gaze. "While I'm sorry that Stephani and Sara were kidnapped and got hurt, I think it was the best thing to ever happen to me." Sliding his gaze back to Leo's eyes, Jerry asked, "Does that make me a bad person?"

"Not at all, Jerry," Leo responded softly. "Because I feel the same way."

Jerry nodded. "Then, if it's okay with you, I'd like you to give me my first kiss." Even as he spoke the words, Jerry's heart rate spiked, anticipation thrumming through him.

Will Leo do it?

Jerry sure hoped so. He didn't know what he would do if Leo said he didn't kiss. Over the years, he'd heard more than one man claim kissing was for women.

"Oh, honey," Leo rumbled, his lips curving into a wide smile even as his eyes narrowed. The feral gleam returned to his expression as he lowered his head and rubbed his cheek against Jerry's own. "I will kiss every inch of your body at some point, my mate," Leo whispered huskily into his ear. "And I'm honored to be your first."

Then Leo turned his head and pressed his lips lightly against the corner of Jerry's mouth in a gentle touch. He lifted, then moved to the other corner of his mouth. Then he licked along Jerry's lower lip before suckling at the flesh lightly.

Jerry gasped at the stimulus, the play sending zings down his chest.

"Yessss," Leo rumbled, then sealed his mouth over Jerry's fully. He dipped his tongue between his lips, teasing at Jerry's own. Pulling away, he peered into Jerry's gaze, smiling at him. "Just follow my lead and enjoy, baby."

Leo threaded the fingers of his left hand into Jerry's hair, tugging the strands lightly and using the hold to tip Jerry's head to the side a little. He dipped his head and sealed his mouth over Jerry's once again. Then he pushed his tongue inside Jerry, using his lips and tongue to massage and manipulate Jerry's own.

Going with it, Jerry twisted his fingers into the back of Leo's shirt. He touched his tongue to Leo's. The move earned him a soft, pleased-sounding growl from the other man.

Jerry lost himself in the sensation of Leo's lips and tongue. His brain shut down. His body felt as if it went up in flames, sending fiery tendrils through him. When his erection began to pulse in time with Leo's laps against his tongue, Jerry groaned and shifted his hips restlessly, his body searching for something.

Through the haze of pleasure, Jerry felt pressure on his crotch. He gasped, then moaned into Leo's kiss. The pressure became a rhythmic massage, and Jerry bucked helplessly into the touch.

Leo broke the kiss, and Jerry gasped, sucking in a deep breath of air he hadn't even realized he'd needed.

"Come for me, mate," Leo purred into his ear. "Don't fight your need." He nipped Jerry's earlobe, then drew it into his mouth for a few light sucks.

The extra stimulus caused a riot in Jerry's mind, and it shut down as it overloaded with ecstasy.

Jerry cried out and bucked. His body erupted in bliss-inducing tingles. He couldn't have stopped himself even if he'd recognized the signs . . . which he didn't.

With a cry, Jerry erupted. His orgasm blind-sided him, causing his senses to sing. Panting harshly, Jerry floated on waves upon waves of blissful endorphins.

He wasn't entirely certain how long he was out of it. When he finally blinked his eyes open, he found a very smug-looking Leo staring down at him. His forefingers petted along his jaw, back and forth.

"So gorgeous in your pleasure," Leo murmured before dipping his head and pecking a kiss to his lips. "Plan to put that expression on your face often."

Jerry gasped softly, trying to catch his breath. He couldn't ever remember an orgasm feeling like that before.

And it's all due to this man . . . this shifter.

God, how did I get so lucky?

Leo teased his fingertips down Jerry's neck. "I'm really enjoying the way you're looking at me right now, Jerry." Cocking his head, he roved his gaze over him. "Care to share your thoughts?"

Feeling a little self-conscious, Leo mumbled, "Just feeling lucky."

"Me, too." Leo pecked another kiss to his lips, then pushed upward, easing from Jerry's grip on his shirt. His attention strayed to where he still ever-so-gently pushed against Jerry's crotch . . . which was now damp. "Can I open your pants and lick you clean?" Leo peered hungrily at Jerry's groin as he licked his lips. "Your cum smells so fucking fantastic. I wanna taste."

"O-Okay." The word was out of Jerry's mouth before his bliss-fried brain could catch up.

Leo growled, the sound one of pure pleasure, then he reached for Jerry's fly.

Unable to help himself, Jerry tensed.

Obviously catching the move, Leo froze, his fingers pausing a hairsbreadth from his zipper. "Baby? Jerry?" He lowered his right hand to Jerry's stomach, sliding it under his coat. "You okay? Talk to me."

Feeling Leo's fingertips tease over the t-shirt covering his belly, Jerry blew out a harsh breath. "S-Sorry. You're fine," he muttered, feeling his cheeks heat. "You just, um—"

Leo continued to tease at his stomach, pushing up his coat. "Talk to me, my lover," he urged while popping the button of his jeans. "Tell me what I did wrong." Even as he slid down Jerry's zipper, he returned his focus to Jerry's face, his expression turning beseeching. "I can't know how to please you if you don't tell me what I did wrong, baby."

"You moved so quickly," Jerry blurted out, feeling his cheeks heat for a reason other than arousal. Hating his fair, redheaded complexion, he grimaced. "Um, fast moves in the past." Pausing, Jerry couldn't continue to hold Leo's gaze. He swallowed hard, all arousal fleeing him. "It meant pain."

"Ahhhh," Leo crooned. "I can't promise I won't always yank you to me or seize your lips." Pulling his hand from Jerry's stomach, Leo moved it to tease at Jerry's lips, redrawing his focus. "But know this. You are my mate, my other half. My reason for living." Leo swept his gaze up and down Jerry's mostly covered form, then returned his attention to Jerry's face, meeting his gaze again. "That means I will never harm you. You're my reason for living. I'll always do anything to protect you."

Overwhelmed by not only the riot of emotions that were surging through him, but by the intensity of Leo's voice, Jerry felt pinpricks hit the backs of his eyes. He swallowed a whimper even as his gut clenched. Turning away from Leo, he scrambled away from him.

"B-Bathroom," Jerry cried before swallowing back another sob. "Pl-Please." That time, he knew he hadn't hidden his overwhelming emotions.

"Yeah, baby," Leo murmured, sounding so damn understanding. "Third door on your right. Head in there, and I'll find you a change of clothes and leave them just outside the door."

Unable to resist the allure of hiding his wayward emotions, Jerry jumped to his feet and rushed from the room, more than happy to hide under the water of a hot, private shower.

CHAPTER SEVEN

Leo bit back a sigh as he watched Jerry run to the bathroom like a jackrabbit fleeing a fox. Rubbing his hand over his face, he did his best to ignore the throb of his unsatisfied cock. He shook his head, knowing he'd pushed his mate too hard too fast.

What the fuck happened to patience?

Yeah, I fucked that up. Now I need to find a way to help my man relax and connect with me.

What could we do to do that though?

Vowing to give it some thought, Leo headed through the house to find Jerry a clean set of clothes. He rummaged through the shopping bags they'd left on the bed earlier and found a pair of jeans and a t-shirt. Even though he remembered Jerry had picked out a package of underwear, Leo didn't bother opening it and grabbing a pair.

If Jerry insisted on wearing them, Leo would start offering them. He hoped his mate wouldn't care, however. As a shifter, Leo didn't bother with them himself, since it was just one more article of clothing that needed to be stripped before changing to his wolf form. Leo knew a lot of shifters that felt the same way. Humans, however, they often found the custom of going commando odd . . . until they mated a shifter and had sex so often that their underwear either got in the way too many times or ended up ruined.

Leo knocked softly on the door. Not expecting an answer, he immediately stated, "I'm setting your clothes on the floor here, Jer. I'll be in the kitchen making dinner." Leo did as he'd said and put the clothes on the floor, then headed to the kitchen. He'd just begun putting away the groceries they'd brought when his sensitive hearing picked up the quiet opening and closing of the bathroom door. A moment later, the shower water started running.

Leo's dick twitched behind his fly. Reaching down, he adjusted himself. The thought of a wet and slippery Jerry caused a bead of pre-cum to ooze from him.

Groaning, Leo realized he needed to think about something else, or his dick would never deflate. For an instant, he thought about slipping into the master bath and rubbing one out. Except, Leo had told Jerry he was making them dinner.

It wasn't that Leo was shy about telling his mate he'd had to go beat off, but he wanted to prove he was a man of his word even more.

To that end, Leo set his mind to ignoring his hard cock and figuring out what to make for dinner. He found the bag of frozen, seasoned curly fries as well as the bag of frozen spicy hot wings. After checking cook times and temperatures, Leo decided he could bake them together.

Leo smiled to himself as he set the oven to preheat, the memory of how Jerry's eyes had lit up when Leo had pointed at the items in the store filling him. His mate had been deprived of many things, fatty, greasy comfort foods being one of them. He intended to help his lover make up for lost time.

While the oven heated, Leo coated a baking sheet with olive oil cooking spray. Then he spread as many wing sections as he could on it without over-crowding it. He grabbed a second sheet, and after spraying that one, too, he spread a massive quantity of curly fries on it.

Leo resealed the packages and put the rest in the freezer for another day . . . or if they wanted to bake seconds. Next, he grabbed a bottle of champagne and popped the cork. He set it on the counter and began searching the cupboards for a pair of flutes.

Just as he located four buried deep in the cupboard, Leo heard the soft footfalls of Jerry's approach. He'd been so busy prepping everything that he hadn't even heard the shower turn off. Grabbing two of the glasses, Leo turned and grinned at his new lover.

"Hey, sweetheart. Water pressure okay?" Leo set the stemware on the counter, then picked up the champagne. "It's been a while since I've been out here." With a shrug, he added, "Don't really remember."

Leo began pouring the drinks, but he spotted Jerry's nod out of the corner of his eye.

"Yeah. It's good." Jerry cleared his throat quietly before saying, "Far better than what was at the warehouse, but that's probably not saying much."

Once done pouring the drinks, Leo put down the champagne and focused on Jerry. He took in the human's tremulous smile and returned it with a sure one of his own. Sliding the champagne flute across the counter toward Jerry, Leo nodded toward the drink.

"Champagne?" Jerry reached out and touched the flute's base, sliding it closer to himself. "What's the occasion?"

"To a new life," Leo replied, picking up his own drink. "To new beginnings." Seeing Jerry's smile grow bigger, Leo decided to tease, "To fucking and bliss and happily ever after."

Jerry's cheeks took on a deep pink glow, and he giggled.

Leo grinned, enjoying the sound.

Yeah, I'm gonna try to pull plenty more of those sounds from my mate.

Nibbling his bottom lip, Jerry focused on the glass as he picked it up. "I've never had alcohol before."

"Really?" The question was out of Leo's mouth before he could think better of it. Not wanting to make it awkward or uncomfortable, he quickly added, "Well, if you don't like the champagne, we can add orange juice to it and make it a mimosa. I know Lark prefers it that way."

"A mimosa?"

Leo nodded as he reached out and clinked his glass to Jerry's. "Yep. He doesn't like beer and wine, but he's a master at creating the fruity alcohol drinks."

Bringing his glass to his lips, Leo took a drink. He watched over the rim of his glass as Jerry did the same. His mate took a tentative sip.

To Leo's delight, Jerry smiled and hummed before taking a bigger drink. Then his mate coughed, his lips curving into a chagrined smile. "Oh, bubbles. Forgot how they stung if you aren't used to them."

Chuckling, Leo nodded. "Like it then?"

Jerry nodded. "Yeah."

"I have several bottles, so feel free to drink as much as you like." Rethinking his words, Leo added, "I'd hate to be the cause of your first hangover though, so, uh . . ."

Laughing softly, Jerry nodded. "Right. That would suck, and I bet I'm a lightweight." He peered down at himself while shaking his head. "I'm skinny and short, so probably can't handle much, huh?"

Leo didn't like the way Jerry seemed to think so little of himself. "I don't know about that." Setting his glass down, he reached for him, resting his hands on Jerry's hips. "While you could use a few more pounds to fill out your frame, I think you're the perfect size." Leo moved in closer, sliding his hands around Jerry's slender frame so he could rest his chin against Jerry's hair, nuzzling the damp strands. "Yes, you definitely feel like the perfect size."

To Leo's pleasure, he felt Jerry wind his arms around his waist. His left palm rested on his lower back as his right pressed the glass against his back.

Leo kissed Jerry's temple before whispering, "Yeah. Perfect."

A second later, Leo felt a tremble work through Jerry's body. That was followed by a hitch and a sniffle. When Jerry pressed his face against Leo's pectoral and shuddered again, Leo frowned.

Dipping his head, Leo kissed Jerry's hairline. At the same time, he rubbed up and down his back. "Easy, baby," he murmured.

In response, Jerry sobbed as he continued to hide his face in Leo's shirt.

"Let it out, Jer," Leo rumbled as he continued to massage Jerry's back. He kept his hands gentle, as well as his tone. "A good cry is cathartic, sweetie."

Bussing a kiss to Jerry's temple, Leo continued to croon encouraging nonsense. He ignored the beep of the oven, telling him it was done pre-heating. Instead, he nuzzled and held his mate, just holding him as he trembled and shook in his arms.

After a good ten minutes, Jerry's breathing evened out. He heaved a huge sigh, then rubbed his face on Leo's shirt. A second later, he jerked his head back.

"Crap," Jerry whispered. Peering up at him through damp lashes with red-rimmed eyes, he appeared so uncertain. "S-Sorry about your shirt."

"It's fine, Jerry." Leo loved the fact that Jerry felt safe enough to fall apart in his arms, even though he hated the things in his lover's life that had caused it. "It's just a shirt. It'll wash."

Jerry's smile appeared tremulous, but at least, he smiled.

Leo reached over and grabbed a box of tissues that had been left on the counter by someone. "Go relax in front of the fire, Jer," he urged. Holding the box out to Jerry, he offered an encouraging smile. "After I put the food in the oven, I'll ditch the shirt, then join you. We'll drink champagne, and we'll talk about anything you want or nothing at all."

Nodding, Jerry eased out of his hold. "Thank you." He glanced at Leo's shirt and grimaced. "I can't believe I did that."

Shrugging, Leo turned and picked up the platter of wings. "There's nothing wrong with crying, Jerry." After putting the food in to cook, he set the timer so he knew when to add the French fries. When he turned back around, Leo saw that Jerry hadn't moved, and he didn't look like he believed him. Resting his right hand on Jerry's shoulder, Leo squeezed lightly. "It's our body's way of purging toxic emotions."

"When was the last time you cried?" Jerry asked.

Leo hummed as he reached for the hem of his polo shirt. After pulling it over his head, he stated, "When my mother died." Thinking quickly, doing figures in his head, Leo came up with, "That would have been eighty-seven years ago in March."

Jerry's eyes widened for a second, but then he seemed to catch himself. "Right. Long life," he whispered. "That'll take some getting used to." Jerry cleared his throat, still looking discomfited. "And that's a legitimate reason."

"So is the return of your life," Leo countered.

Unwilling to argue with his mate, Leo pressed a kiss to Jerry's temple, then headed toward the laundry room, which was attached to the other side of the kitchen. He dropped his shirt on the floor in front of the washer, then returned to the kitchen. To Leo's relief, he saw that Jerry had finally headed into the living room.

Leo grabbed his glass of champagne as well as the bottle. He carried both to the living room and, after taking a sip from his glass, placed both on a side table. Smiling at Jerry as he passed him, Leo took in the way he sat curled up on the sofa, his legs tucked under him. His mate rested the tissue box beside his knee and had a few crinkled up on his lap. Jerry held his nearly empty champagne flute in his left hand, resting the base on his thigh. After Leo added another log to the fire, he joined him, grabbing the items he'd left on the side table first.

After easing onto the sofa next to Jerry, Leo topped off his mate's glass before doing the same with his own. Then he placed the bottle on the floor nearby. Leaning back against the cushion, he let out a long sigh.

"This is a comfortable sofa," Leo commented absently. Staring at the ceiling, he wiggled a little, rubbing his back against it. "Whoever picked it out has good taste. I'm glad they didn't take it with them."

"You said this place had been rented for a while?"

Turning his head on the back of the cushion, Leo smiled at Jerry. "Yeah. A group of flying shifters that Alpha Declan and his people rescued from some asshole scientist's facility." Leo growled under his breath. "The douche bag was doing experiments on them and trying to create super soldiers or something like that."

"Oh wow," Jerry muttered, his eyes widening with his surprise. "No wonder you guys didn't have any trouble tracking down Stephani and Sara and taking out the gang."

Leo chuckled, grinning. "Yeah. Oh, speaking of the gangs." Straightening and shifting his weight to the left, he pulled his phone from his belt clip. "Hold this." After handing off his champagne flute, Leo began flipping through screens on his phone until he pulled up the article he wanted. Then he traded his phone for his glass, showing it to Jerry.

"Gang war culminates in explosion, destroying both sides," Jerry read the headline. Gaping, he snapped his gaze to Leo. "Gang war? Explosion?"

Still grinning, Leo shrugged. "The news article is bogus,

of course, but yeah. Jared wiped out both the gangs and blew up their buildings."

"Jared?" Jerry tipped his head. "He's the guy who pistol-whipped Myron, right?"

Leo nodded. "Yep. I don't know too much of his history, but I know he's an expert marksman, martial artist, and explosives specialist. If I didn't know he doesn't take authority well, I would have pegged him as ex-military." Smirking, he took his phone back from Jerry before tossing it on the side table. "I'm thinking a line of work that was a little darker before he hooked up with Carson, but since he's on our side, I don't ask questions."

"What kind of shifter is he?" Jerry asked curiously before taking a sip of his drink. "I know you're a wolf, and you said some fliers lived here. How many different kinds are there?"

The oven timer beeped, so Leo rose as he explained. "Jared is a human. Carson is a wolf shifter, like most of the shifters in this area. There's a tiger and elephant around here, along with a black panther and a komodo dragon. The fliers were all different and on the smaller side." Leo placed the fries in the oven below the wings, taking a second to check their progress as well. After shutting the door, he returned to the sofa while admitting, "I think one of them mated a bear, then they all moved when another in the flock discovered his mate was a lion who is on the council."

"Council?"

Resting back on the sofa, Leo nodded. "Shifter Council." He curled his lip as he added, "They're supposed to be in charge of policing alphas and keeping our species safe and a secret, but we discovered at least one of them was actually selling shifters to the scientists." Shaking his head, Leo told him, "The asshole is currently on the run, at the moment, but there's people tracking him."

Jerry rested a hand on his forearm in an obvious attempt

to soothe. "It sounds like your world is just as dangerous as mine was."

"It's your world, too, now, Jerry," Leo gently corrected, resting his free hand over his mate's. "And I'll keep you safe. You have my word."

Jerry smiled back at him. "Thanks."

CHAPTER EIGHT

"Where are we going?" Jerry asked, peering out the window at the snow-laden trees. "What adventure do you have for us today?"

"Today, we're going to the home of Frankie and Vince." Leo grinned at him and squeezed Jerry's thigh where he rested his right hand. "And it's a surprise."

Over the last four days, Leo had treated him to a new activity every day.

They'd gone to the movies, which had been fun . . . and different than he remembered—the seats more comfortable and the popcorn bags bigger. They'd tried skiing the next day, but Jerry had figured out pretty quickly that going that fast down a hill while standing on long, thin pieces of wood terrified him. Since they'd already been bundled up, they'd switched to sledding, instead.

On another day, Leo had taken him to Colin City, and they'd walked the town. He pointed out different places and talked about different jobs. Jerry had mostly listened, trying to figure out if anything interested him. It had been a bit boring, but he understood the necessity of it.

His favorite times, however, were when they would get back to the house. They would cook together, then eat in front of the fire. Sometimes they would watch television. Jerry found the educational shows Leo favored interesting.

Regardless of where they were or what they were doing, Leo often touched him. In public, he would hold his hand and press a kiss to his temple. In private, he would wrap his arms around him and take his mouth in deep kisses that left Jerry panting and hard.

Unfortunately, Leo hadn't taken it further than that again. He seemed to be waiting for something. Jerry just wasn't certain what.

"Oh, I should warn you before we get there," Leo began, squeezing Jerry's thigh to gain his attention. "Vince is a vampire."

"Oh, wow."

"He's a decent guy, and totally devoted to Frankie and their son, Freddie."

"They have a son?" Jerry didn't know what to think of that. "But they're both guys, so how did that work? Did they adopt? That's allowed?"

As soon as the words were out of his mouth, Jerry realized how ridiculous that sounded. He placed his hand over Leo's and squeezed. "Sorry. Guess you probably think I'm stuck in the Stone Age, huh?" Feeling a little overwhelmed, Jerry admitted, "I was raised pretty isolated. This" — he squeezed Leo's hand where they rested on his thigh — "is taking some getting used to."

Oh, that's what he's waiting for. For me to be comfortable with the idea of us together.

While Jerry had been a whore for almost six years, that was so very different than what Leo was asking from him. He'd been forced into it. His body had been used by others, and he hadn't had a choice.

Leo wants me to choose him.

"It just means you've been sheltered and been given misinformation."

Jerry snapped his focus back to Leo, wondering what he'd missed. The shifter glanced his way and winked. "Artificial insemination and surrogates are very popular with shifters. They used Frankie's seed, so their little boy will be a shifter once he hits puberty."

"Wow." Jerry barked a soft laugh, then grinned at Leo. "I'm saying that a lot."

Leo chuckled and shrugged. "That's okay. You're going through an adjustment."

Jerry nodded. Amazement filled him, as it often did, at how patient and understanding Leo was. He knew the man wanted him, and now that he'd figured out what the shifter was waiting on, he intended to do something about it.

Because I want him, too. I just have to figure out how to express myself.

Having never had to make the first move before, Jerry wasn't entirely sure how to do that.

Leo slowing the truck, then turning it into a plowed driveway pulled Jerry out of his musings. A home appeared between the trees, but Leo bypassed it, taking a branch off to the left which led to a small barn. There was a taller structure a few feet behind it.

"Here we are," Leo stated needlessly, a wide grin splitting his lips, and he parked and shut off the truck. "Come on."

Jerry followed, shoving his hands in his coat's pockets to ward off the winter chill. He hurried after Leo, who was walking half-turned and beckoning to him. Once he reached Leo, Jerry grabbed his outstretched hand and squeezed.

That simple action earned him a huge smile.

"So, can vampires come out in daylight?" Jerry asked, curious to see if any of the myths were correct.

"Yes," a cultured, slightly accented voice replied. A slender, light-brown-haired man stepped out of the recesses of the barn. He sported a smile, so Jerry hoped he hadn't offended the stranger. "I'm Vince." He held out his hand. "Welcome to my home."

Jerry took Vince's hand. "Nice to meet you."

After a quick shake, Vince released him, then grinned at Leo. "Frankie's inside. We have everything ready."

Unable to help himself, Jerry gasped. "You have fangs."

Vince returned his attention back to Jerry, amusement etched on his features. "Vampire, remember?" Leading the way inside the small, clean barn, he continued, "Pretty much whatever myths you can think of about us, they aren't true. Most of us love garlic. Going into a church won't strike us dead, and neither does sunlight." Chuckling softly, Vince focused on Jerry as he walked and added, "And we don't turn into bats."

Jerry laughed. "No, shifters do that."

Vince nodded, chuckling. "Indeed."

Turning to the right through an opening between stalls, Vince led the way into a large, indoor arena. "Here we are." He pointed. "That's my beloved, Frankie, and our son, Freddie. When we started tacking up Charger and Bailey, he insisted on riding, too. Don't worry," he added with a wink. "We'll keep him out of your way."

"Riding?" Jerry felt his heart rate spike in his chest as excitement surged through him. He tore his gaze away from where a huge, dirty-blond haired guy kept an eye on a toddler riding a small horse. Peering to the left, Jerry just resisted the urge to do a happy dance.

Two horses were saddled, bridled, and tied to a hitching post along the arena's left wall.

Whipping his attention to Leo, Jerry whispered, "How did you know?"

To Jerry's surprise, he saw Leo's cheeks pinken. The bigger man squeezed Jerry's hand as he cleared his throat. "Well, before meeting you, I did a bit of research on you, and I saw an article about you winning second place in high school rodeo." Leo waved his free hand toward Vince and Frankie. "These guys are one of the few in the pack who have horses, and since they built an indoor arena last year, I thought you might enjoy it."

"God, yes," Jerry burst out. He didn't know what to think

about Leo researching him, so decided to think about it another time. Instead, he dwelled on the incredibly awesome and thoughtful thing Leo had done for him. "I missed Jericho so bad over the years."

"Jericho?" Leo asked as he guided him toward the pair of saddled horses.

"My gelding," Jerry told him. "I bought him as a two-year-old and broke him." Pausing next to the paint horse, he slowly lifted his hand, allowing the horse to sniff his fingers. "If I'd known I was coming, I would have brought you something, big boy."

"I thought of that." Leo pulled several baby carrots out of his coat pocket. "Here."

"Aww, thanks." Jerry beamed a smile at Leo, appreciating his forethought. Taking the offered carrots, he turned and held them up for the horse. "Here ya go, handsome."

The horse sniffed at the offered items, then swiftly lipped them from his fingers.

Realizing he should have asked permission, Jerry turned and gazed at the vampire. Fortunately, the slender male appeared amused more than anything else. Still, Jerry knew he should apologize if Vince had a rule about not feeding the horse when it had a bit in its mouth. Some people were very strict about it.

"Uh, hope that was okay that I fed them while they have their bridles on." Jerry felt his cheeks heat. "I apologize for not asking permission."

Vince laughed softly, shaking his head. "Don't even worry about it. I know where the horses were trained have the rule where they don't feed the horse while tacked up, but that was the first thing Frankie changed." Vince turned and peered at the big male who was still keeping close to the youngster on the small horse that Jerry guessed from his size and coloring to be a Pony of America. The kid was doing a damn fine job of trotting figure eights under the watchful eye of his father. He guessed the boy had been riding since before he was old enough to walk.

A pang of kinship shot through him.

Damn. Kinship with a little wolf kid because of a horse. I like these people.

"When was the last time you rode?" Vince asked, sweeping his gaze up and down Jerry's frame.

Jerry would have felt disconcerted by the perusal, but then the vampire stepped close to the saddle and began adjusting the length of the stirrup. Pulling his head together, Jerry rounded the animal and began to do the same. He unbuckled the leather strap around the lengths of leather under the wide fender flap, then slid the metal keeper up so he could pull the clasp out of the holes.

"What are you moving it to?" Jerry asked, glancing over the saddle at Vince.

"Up four holes," the vampire replied. "After that, check it and let me know if it's where you like the length."

Nodding, Jerry did as he'd been told. As he placed the metal tabs in the holes, then slid the keeper back into position, he told the man, "I was kicked out of my home over eight years ago. I managed to live the first couple of years on the streets just fine, but then the gang picked me up." Jerry lifted the stirrup to his armpit and stuck out his arm, measuring the length by resting his fingertips on the side of the saddle. "Up one more hole. I like a bit shorter than is traditional." Smirking, Jerry added with a shrug, "I mowed lawns during the summer to earn cash for riding lessons, but the only training barn in the area gave English lessons."

"Oh, gods," Vince muttered, although he smiled as he did it. "Don't tell Frankie or he's going to ask you to help him learn how to jump. He's become obsessed with it."

Jerry laughed. "Oh, so you mean if I open a riding and lesson stable around here, I'd already have one student?"

"Absolutely," the vampire replied.

To Jerry's surprise, the man appeared deadly serious . . . although he appeared happy about it, too.

Huh. There's an idea.

"I'll, uh . . . I'll give it some thought," Jerry admitted as he finished adjusting the stirrup. Smiling at the other man, he stated, "First, I better see how much I remember."

"These two horses are Morgans. This one is Bailey. That's Charger," he said, pointing at the dark bay horse behind him. "Both are what are called push button horses."

Jerry lifted his hand and gave a thumbs up, indicating he understood. A push button horse was one which was very soft-sided, responsive, and very well trained. It would do its best to obey as long as it understood the request.

"Cool. I really appreciate you agreeing to let me and Leo ride them."

Vince smirked as he offered a single nod. "Have fun," he offered just as his Freddie yelled, "Daddy, watch!"

As Jerry started to round the horse again—Bailey—he found himself caught by Leo. The shifter wrapped an arm around him and tugged him close. Dipping his head, he sealed his mouth over Jerry's.

Gripping Leo's jacket, Jerry quickly opened to him. He slid his tongue out and teased it along Leo's own. His blood had a predictable reaction, just as it did every time he was kissed by Leo. It heated and flowed south, pooling in his groin.

Leo groaned and lifted his head, ending the kiss. "Damn it," he grumbled. "That was supposed to be a chaste, let's go have fun kiss." While Leo scowled at him, there was mirth filling his eyes. "Now I gotta ride with a boner."

Jerry's jaw sagged open, and he found himself looking down and spotting the impressive bulge behind Leo's fly. "I-I did that? With just a kiss?" Tearing his gaze away from the enticing sight, he found Leo's gaze again.

"Baby, just looking at you does this to me," Leo admitted with a wry smile. He shrugged. "You're my mate."

The simple statement firmed Jerry's resolve to figure out how to make the first move. He wanted what Leo offered. Jerry just needed to decide how to make it happen.

"Then let's enjoy this amazing opportunity you set up for me, Leo," Jerry murmured, lifting his left hand to trace over Leo's jaw. Girding up his courage, he decided to try his hand at being forward. "Then we can go home and take care of that." Jerry cast a quick glance down at Leo's fly so his meaning would be clear.

Leo groaned, the sound full of husky need. "Damn it, baby," he whined. "That's not gonna help."

Jerry couldn't help himself. He laughed as he stepped away from Leo. Reaching down, he adjusted his own mostly hard dick.

"At least we're in the same boat," Jerry admitted, fighting against the heat rising in his cheeks.

"Get on the horse," Leo ordered roughly. "Let's see what ya got."

Grinning, Leo rounded the horse. As he did a quick, one last check over the tack, he asked, "When was the last time you rode a horse? Or do you do it often?"

Leo sighed deeply, then turned back to his own horse. "Actually, it's probably been around sixty years or so, so I'm probably going to be a little rusty."

"That's okay," Jerry replied before unclipping the lead rope from the halter and gathering his reins. "It's been years for me, too. We'll warm up together."

With that thought, Jerry lifted his left foot to the stirrup and with a small bounce, swung into the saddle. He settled lightly on the western saddle's seat, appreciating how well trained the horse was as it waited patiently for him to get situated. Finding his right stirrup, he straightened.

For the first time in what felt like forever, Jerry found himself feeling relaxed and at home. He positioned his hand on the reins, which caught the horse's attention. Jerry noticed how it shifted its weight just a little as it flicked an ear in his direction while turning its head a smidge to peer at him with one eye.

Leaning down, Jerry stroked the animal's neck. After confirming that Leo was comfortable and ready, Jerry guided the horse along the rail of the indoor arena.

Over the course of the next couple of hours, Jerry felt long dormant muscles awaken as he recalled the thrill of becoming one with his mount.

Chapter Nine

Leo did his best to hide his arousal . . . and anticipation. While he'd always found Jerry attractive, he hadn't realized he could find his mate even more stunning. When his man got around horses, however, Jerry took on a bearing that radiated confidence which was sexy as fuck.

Due to that, Leo had sported a boner through the entire experience. That was okay, though, because he would give anything, handle any discomfort, to see that kind of happiness flooding his mate. Leo knew getting a pair of horses was in their future, maybe even more than a couple.

"Thank you so much for that, Leo," Jerry stated, leaning on the middle consul. The man still seemed to glow with his joy. "I can't begin to explain how much I'd missed horseback riding."

"I could tell." Leo liked the way that Jerry reached out and placed his hand on his thigh. He settled his own hand over his mate's and squeezed lightly. "You practically glowed. It was obvious you were in your element. Are you thinking about getting one?" Grinning widely, Leo couldn't help but offer, "We could get a couple and ride together. You could ride with Vince or Frankie, too, if I'm working."

Jerry's brows furrowed. While some of the excited light dimmed from his eyes, his jaw seemed to firm up with resolve. "Actually, I was thinking about getting a part-time job, so I had money to get my GED. I never finished high school, since—" Jerry grimaced, then continued, "Well, since I was kicked out by my parents for being gay."

Leo's heart rate spiked. That was the first time Jerry had actually admitted his sexuality—at least, as far as Leo knew. Well, Leo supposed Jerry could have admitted it out loud when he'd been kicked out.

I will never make him feel that sharing his sexuality will cause him pain again.

Parking in front of their home, Leo squeezed Jerry's hand, then shut off the machine. "I was thinking chili cheese dogs with more of those curly fries you love for a late lunch." They'd been riding longer than Leo had planned, since his mate had been having so much fun.

Jerry groaned and licked his lips. "With relish? And mustard?"

Leo laughed. He loved watching Jerry enjoy what he cooked for him. "Hell, yeah. Is there another way?" It was another rare time when Jerry allowed his inhibitions to ease and he showed his true reactions.

I won't stop raining my mate with affection and care until he's like that all the time. And I won't stop then, either.

"Come on, my mate," Leo urged, pushing his door open. "Let's get inside."

"How about you start the fire while I get everything started in the kitchen?" Jerry offered, falling into step beside Leo as they exited the detached garage and headed to their cabin's front door. "Do you like your hot dogs boiled or is microwaving them okay?"

"I'm pretty damn hungry, so if you want to cut corners and microwave them, that's fine with me," Leo replied, liking the idea of a late lunch in front of the fire. That his mate wanted to prepare a meal for him also appealed to his wolf. "After I get the fire started, I'll come in and help."

Jerry reached out and took Leo's hand, pulling his attention away from where he was sorting his keys in search of the one for the front door. It was only the second time Jerry had initiated contact with him. The move caused his heart rate to spike and his pulse to pound.

"You don't have to, Leo," Jerry told him, his tone taking on a husky note. "Let me do this for you."

"Okay." Leo agreed readily, then brought Jerry's fingers to his lips before teasing, "My legs could use a rest after the workout you put them through."

Jerry laughed, the sound one of joy. "It was fun. Thanks for letting us stay out so long."

"It was truly my pleasure." Then Leo opened the front door and drew his mate inside.

Leo closed the door behind them before stomping his feet on the mat, knocking off some of the snow from his boots. Releasing Jerry, he bent so he could remove them. Stepping onto the hardwood floor in his stocking feet, Leo set his boots on the rack. After that, he pulled off his coat and placed it on a hook hung on the wall.

From the corner of his eye, Leo saw Jerry copying his actions. He appreciated that, since it cut down on water, snow, and mud being tracked through the house. Of course, since Jerry was the one who did most of the cleaning—*gods bless him*—Leo wouldn't have complained anyway.

Leo headed to the living room and started the fire. Within half a minute, he heard Jerry begin puttering around the kitchen. He smiled to himself, relishing the domesticity of it.

The idea of doing the same in Leo's own home crossed his mind. He hadn't voiced it, yet, but he would need to get back to work before too long. Leo knew that everyone from the pack was back in Stone Ridge except Jared and Carson. They were still in San Francisco keeping an eye on the fallout from taking out the gangs.

Once Leo had finished building up the fire, he headed to the back door. He took a few minutes to bring in a couple of armloads of firewood from the back porch. In the process, it soaked his socks, so when he was finished, he yanked them off and left them in the laundry room. Then Leo washed up for supper and returned to the living room.

Groaning softly, more from the pain in his always hard dick than from the twinge in his leg muscles, Leo flopped onto the sofa. He turned his head and watched his mate. The bar that was separating the space cut off the lower half of Leo's view, but that didn't matter. He saw all of him in his mind's eye.

Watching Jerry glide around the kitchen, humming to himself, sent a fresh surge of arousal through Leo's body. He reached down and palmed his erection through his jeans. Fighting back a groan, he struggled to calm down.

At some point, Leo must have closed his eyes, for the next thing he knew, Jerry's soft hand rubbed over his shoulder as he whispered into his ear, "That looks like it hurts. Can I help?"

Leo's breath caught in his chest as he peered up at Jerry. Seeing the lust swirling in his mate's eyes, Leo found it difficult to find his tongue. He saw the way Jerry's eyes were heavy-lidded and how his bottom lip was damp and slightly puffy, as if he'd been nibbling on it.

"Oh, Jerry," Leo rumbled, his desire filling his voice. "There is nothing I would like more." A quick glance to the left showed him where his mate had left the tray of food on the side table. "But if we start that now, those delicious-looking chili dogs will be cold by the time I'm done with you."

Jerry tilted his head to the side as a cheeky grin curved his lips. "Well, we wouldn't want that, would we?"

When Jerry straightened and returned to the tray, Leo groaned. He wanted to kick himself. Why the hell hadn't he just said *hell yes*, grabbed his mate, and not let him go?

Still, Leo held his peace, watching his young mate pick up the tray and carry it closer. He settled it onto the sofa to

Leo's left. Then, to Leo's surprise, Jerry gripped his shoulder again before climbing onto his lap, straddling his thighs.

Leo instinctively grabbed Jerry's hips as he sucked in a surprised breath. Jerry's smile turned shy even as he slid close, pushing his groin against Leo's. The pressure of his sweet mate's hard dick pressing against his own caused his breath to leave him in a harsh, shocked hiss.

"J-Jerry?" Leo couldn't believe the stammer, but he was struggling to pull a single thought into his head.

"Yeah?" Jerry asked, his voice sounding as breathless as Leo felt. Before Leo could come up with something, Jerry turned and grabbed a napkin, then placed a chili dog on it. Straightening again, Jerry brought it to Leo's lips. "Bite."

His mate's movement caused light stimulating friction to Leo's trapped erection. He moaned, which opened his mouth. When Jerry touched the end of the chili dog to his lips, Leo obeyed his sexy human.

The sweetness of the relish burst across his tongue, combining with the spiciness of the mustard, the smoothness of the chili, and the flavor of the beef and bun. It took every bit of his control to chew and swallow, especially when he watched Jerry bring the dog to his own mouth and take a bite. On top of that, his mate continued to hold his gaze through the whole process—oh, and Jerry rocked his hips ever-so-slightly.

"Jerry!" Leo whined as soon as his mouth was empty.

Jerry responded by returning the dog to Leo's mouth. Knowing what was expected, Leo took another bite . . . a big one, because he wanted—hell, *needed*—the food to be finished damn fast.

Before taking another bite of his own, Jerry whispered, "Gotta eat, or we won't have the strength we need for a very fun afternoon and evening."

Leo loved the sound of that. "Hell yeah," he muttered as

soon as he could, then he took the last bite of the dog, nipping Jerry's fingers in the process. When Jerry picked up the second chili dog and took the first bite, Leo moaned. "Gods, it's so fucking sexy the way you eat."

Grinning around his mouthful, Jerry fed Leo another bite. It didn't take them long to polish off the second chili dog. Then Jerry lifted the glass of bubbling liquid that contained a straw. He guided it to Leo's mouth, and Leo obliged by taking a sip. The sweet tang of *Sprite*—Jerry's drink of choice—burst across his tongue.

All the while Jerry had been feeding Leo, he'd kept up a light rocking. Or that could have been Leo and his hands on Jerry's hips. He couldn't let his little man go . . . not now that he had him where he wanted him—warm and willing against him.

Finally, Jerry placed the cup back on the tray.

Leo's patience broke. He didn't give him time to grab anything else. Instead, he slid his hands around and cradled the globes of Jerry's ass in each palm. Planting his feet, he rutted his hips up while pulling Jerry tighter against him.

Jerry gasped, and unable to resist the allure of his mate's sweet mouth, Leo leaned forward and captured it with his own. Thrusting his tongue into Jerry's mouth, he lapped at his mate's slick appendage. Leo fed his lover a groan as his balls began to tingle and tighten.

It had been too long, and his control was shot. As soon as Leo felt Jerry's arms wind around his neck, his testicles contracted. Moaning into Jerry's mouth, reveling in the feel of his human plastered against him, warm and pliant in his arms, Leo gave himself over to his need.

Leo's orgasm swelled through his system. Sweet bliss swamped his senses. His cock unloaded, throbbing and twitching, filling his crotch with his seed.

Continuing to rock against Jerry, Leo relished the aftershocks. Suddenly, Jerry broke the kiss and buried his face against Leo's neck. He whimpered as he shook in Leo's hold, and the salty scent of his mate's release flooded the air.

Growling with his pleasure, Leo stilled his movements. He forced his fingers to ease their grip. Lightly massaging one cheek, he skimmed his left hand up Jerry's back, gently tracing over the knobs of his spine.

"Gods, Jer," Leo mumbled, his voice rough even to his own ears. "That was the sexiest fucking thing . . . ever." Feeling the wet, seed-soaked material around his still-hard dick, Leo chuckled huskily. "Love that you get me so hot I can't even think long enough to take our clothes off."

Jerry giggled softly against Leo's shirt. "Are you gonna make it a habit of messing up my pants?"

Loving that sound, Leo dipped his head and nibbled at Jerry's neck as he whispered, "Probably. That okay with you?"

Lifting his head, Jerry met his gaze. He swallowed hard enough to cause his Adam's apple to bob before he stated, "Only if you help clean up."

Leo growled as he grinned. From the way Jerry's eyes widened, he knew he sported a feral, hungry look. "Hell yeah, baby."

Without waiting for a response from Jerry, Leo returned his grip to his mate's hips. He rocked forward, but instead of standing, he immediately sank to his knees. Taking his human with him, Leo urged Jerry to sprawl on the rug before the fire.

"Stay right there, baby," Leo ordered. "While I go grab lube."

Jerry nodded, a satisfied smile curving his lips. He even went so far as to put his hands behind his head and spread his legs a little. The move put his lean, toned body on magnificent display, the wet spot on the front of his jeans drawing Leo's attention to his trapped, still-hard dick.

Moaning, Leo muttered, "Gods, you're a minx."

As Leo crossed to the fire and added a couple more logs, he noticed the way Jerry nibbled his lower lip and how his scent of satisfaction suddenly became tinged by uncertainty. Not liking that in the least little bit, Leo dropped to one knee beside his shoulder and rested his hand near Jerry's head.

After pressing a swift, hard kiss to Jerry's lips, Leo lifted his head and stated, "Just so you know, I like that about you." He kissed Jerry again before winking and adding, "Very much."

Relief filled Leo when he once again scented renewed pleasure and arousal from Jerry. After giving his mate another kiss, he rose again. Leo strode swiftly to his bedroom and yanked open his nightstand drawer. Even as he grabbed the lube, he prayed he wasn't jumping the gun. Just because Jerry had finally come to him, had acknowledged their connection, Leo didn't know if that meant he was ready to bond.

Please be ready to bond.

Leo took a deep, settling breath, mentally vowing to go at whatever speed Jerry wanted. Then he hurried back to the living room. When he reached there, Leo nearly swallowed his tongue.

In the short time he'd been out of the room, Jerry had stripped completely. His sexy mate lay sprawled just where he'd left him, sans clothes, and with his legs splayed. With his hands back behind his head, Jerry peered at Leo from beneath his lashes. He had just the faintest of treasure trails beneath his belly button which led to a carefully trimmed thatch of curls and a long, slender prick—both of which were still covered with dabs of Jerry's cum.

Leo's mouth watered.

"Oh, baby," Leo whispered, dropping the lube on the rug nearby as he reached for the hem of his shirt. "Please tell me you're ready to be mine."

Jerry smiled sweetly. "I'm ready to be yours, mate."

On a moan, Leo stripped.

Chapter Ten

Jerry watched with bated breath as Leo revealed his body to him. He'd seen the man without a shirt plenty of times over the last few days. Finally, he would see the rest of him.

His breath hitching, Jerry swallowed hard as Leo carefully parted his damp fly, revealing his long, thick cock. He guessed the shifter to be in the nine-inch range with plenty of girth. Jerry's asshole clenched as anticipation filled him.

Never before had he wanted a dick in his ass, but right then, he couldn't think of anything he wanted more.

Leo bending and shoving off his jeans broke Jerry's view of his gorgeous erection. Returning his focus to his lover's face, he swallowed hard, trying to get some saliva to his suddenly dry throat. The look of desire, of *need*, that practically glowed in Leo's eyes took Jerry's breath away.

This shifter doesn't just want me — he craves *me.*

A feeling of warmth bloomed in Jerry's chest. While he thought it was too early to love the man that lowered to his hands and knees and crawled between his legs, he knew he was well on his way. Reaching for the man, Jerry allowed his emotions to bleed through onto his face.

Leo met Jerry's gaze and moaned. "Jerry," he crooned before lowering his head and licking a stripe up Jerry's erection. He hummed. "So damn good."

Jerry gasped, his hands clenching in Leo's thick dirty-blond hair. "Leo!"

No one had ever offered to suck Jerry's dick before, and the hot, warm swipes of Leo's tongue caused his abdominals to clench, and tingles erupted over his chest. His nipples beaded, and his breath caught in his throat.

The sensation was decadent, thrilling his body and sending a haze of bliss over his senses. Groaning and arching, he shuddered and twitched. Unable to help himself, he tightened his hold in Leo's hair as he whimpered his lover's name mixed with pleas, but for what, he didn't know.

"I got you, my sweet," Leo crooned, the sound vibrating Jerry's balls. "Just let go and feel." Then he swiped his tongue over his soft sack, and Jerry could do nothing but obey.

His balls pulled tight, his orgasm blindsiding him. Leo must have been expecting it, for he wrapped his lips around Jerry's crown even before his first shot burst from him. His lover's gentle sucks to his flared flesh ripped a scream from Jerry's throat as he came . . . and came.

Jerry soared on heady waves of endorphins as Leo continued to pleasure his groin. It wasn't until his shifter eased off his cock that Jerry realized the man also had a finger — wait, no two — in his ass. He clenched on instinct.

"Easy, my mate," Leo rumbled huskily. "Stay relaxed for me."

As Leo spoke, he rubbed against that pleasure-inducing bump that so few had bothered to find. Jerry gasped as fiery tingles shot through his rectum. Leo didn't just glance off it, either . . . he worked it — massaging, bumping, and nudging. Goose bumps broke out over his groin, heat spiraling through him, causing his arousal to surge once more.

"L-Leo," Jerry whined. "H-How?"

Jerry wasn't certain what he was asking, but Leo seemed to understand.

"That's the way, Jer," Leo urged, nuzzling his hard dick with his nose. "Gonna slide a third one in now. Push out." Then he wrapped his lips around Jerry's crown, suckling lightly as he lapped his tongue over his glans.

Holy shit! How can I be hard again?

Leo chuckled around his mouthful, peering at him with smug satisfaction in his eyes. He popped off just long enough to mutter, "We've been dancing around each other for days, my mate. We're both on edge with our need. We'll both be ready to go many times this night." Then he stuck out his tongue and tickled Jerry's frenulum before tipping his head and lightly sucking on the bit of wrinkled flesh.

Jerry vaguely realized he'd asked the question out loud, but he was immediately swamped with waves of ecstasy that shut down any hope of thought. Even the increased stretch to his chute didn't ease his burgeoning need. His desire swelled again, and his thighs trembled.

"L-Leo," Jerry cried, uncertainty flooding him. The blood in his body felt as if it burned through his veins, and the muscles in his limbs shook. Never had he experienced anything even close to what surged through him, and he didn't know how to respond. "P-Please. I-I—Leo?"

"You're okay, Jer," Leo crooned after easing off Jerry's dick. "Take slow deep breaths for me."

As Leo spoke, he slipped his fingers out of Jerry's channel. Levering over him, Leo rested his weight on his left hand as he gripped Jerry's upper thigh with his right. Leo peered down at him with an intense gaze.

"Remember to push out, sweetheart," Leo reminded as he nudged his cock against Jerry's hole, which suddenly felt oddly empty. "It'll help you stay relaxed and more comfortable."

Wish someone had told me that years ago.

"Hey." Leo bussed a kiss to the corner of Jerry's mouth, redrawing his focus. "Stay with me. Focus on me."

Jerry opened eyelids he hadn't realized he'd closed. Staring up into Leo's hazel eyes, he found a gleam of concern there. Lines of strain filled the shifter's features as he held his position.

"If you're not ready, baby. We'll wait. We'll spend the evening pleasing each other in other ways." Leo made the offer, but Jerry could see the torment in his eyes. "Your needs come first. Always."

Jerry knew Leo believed his words. He also realized the shifter would do it. Even though he had his hard dick poised at Jerry's entrance, he would pull away.

As much as Jerry feared that feeling Leo's dick inside his body would bring back all his memories of others, he knew he needed this. On top of that, Jerry wanted what Leo offered. He wanted to be Leo's mate . . . in all ways.

"Take me, Leo," Jerry blurted out.

"Are you certain?"

Nodding, Jerry slid his hands down Leo's skull to his neck, then to his shoulders. He massaged Leo's flesh, admiring his strength. His resolve firmed as he peered into his lover's worried gaze, and he knew he was making the right choice.

"I'm certain, my mate," Jerry replied, loving the way Leo's face flushed and his eyes dilated even more when he said that word. Lifting his right leg, Jerry hitched it over Leo's waist. "Please. I need you."

Leo moaned, the sound deep and rough. "As I need you."

Jerry reveled in Leo's words, hearing the deep ring of truth in them. This shifter would do anything for him. He fully intended to return that gift.

Feeling the pressure of Leo's crown against his hole, Jerry pushed out. He focused on breathing and on his lover's face. To his surprise, the stretch wasn't like he remembered . . . or maybe that was because of who he was with.

"Yes, baby," Leo said on a groan. His eyes narrowed, and beads of sweat broke out on his brow. He continued to ease into Jerry, slow and steady. "Feel so good," he muttered brokenly as he began withdrawing. Before Leo's prick slipped out, he reversed again, pushing back into him. "Jerry!"

Jerry tightened his hold on Leo's shoulders, pulling him close. "Yes, Leo." He held his lover's gaze. "I need you in me. Make me yours."

"You're mine," Leo vowed, growling as he narrowed his eyes. "Never doubt that."

With those words, Leo began moving in earnest. He pushed in and pulled out, speeding up, and with each glide, he rubbed over Jerry's prostate. When Jerry opened his mouth on a groan of pleasure, Leo captured his lips, swallowing the noise and feeding him some moans of his own.

Clinging to Leo, Jerry gave himself over to everything Leo made him feel. His body hummed, his blood fired through him, and his dick throbbed. Jerry rocked into each of Leo's thrusts, digging his heels into his lover's back.

On a whine, Leo broke the kiss. He moved his mouth to Jerry's neck where it met his shoulder. Sucking and laving over the flesh there, Leo caused a new wave of tingles to erupt down Jerry's torso.

"L-Leo!" Jerry cried, feeling his balls begin to tighten once more. "Oh, god!"

"Do it," Leo snarled as he began grunting with each thrust, vocalizing his own enjoyment. "Do it now. Show me you're mine."

When Leo moved his hand from Jerry's left thigh and slipped it between them to grip his dick, Jerry could do nothing but obey. He arched his neck, crying his shifter's name as his dick unloaded once more. Dark spots danced behind Jerry's eyes as his body struggled to process the ecstasy Leo offered him.

"Mine!" Leo roared as he shoved deep and froze.

Jerry gasped as wet heat filled him deep inside. He

moaned, his chute still clenching and releasing spastically from his own release. Never had he felt so connected to another.

"Yours," he whispered, unable to keep the word inside.

Leo moaned again, then sank his teeth into the flesh he'd been working.

A spike of pain stabbed through Jerry's shoulder, and he opened his mouth to gasp. In the next instant, the most amazing zings of ecstasy crashed through him. The spots behind his eyes spread, and his last thought was, what the hell just happened?

Moaning softly, Jerry struggled to get his eyes to open. He became aware of a warm hand rubbing over his stomach before he managed it. Smiling, he let out a long, relaxed sigh.

Jerry found his focus on the fireplace. He was lying on his side, Leo spooned up behind him. The heat of the flames warmed his naked front while his lover did the same to his back.

"Mmm, welcome back." Leo nipped his neck over where he'd bitten, causing the hairs on Jerry's nape to stand on end. "I was getting worried."

"Sorry," Jerry whispered, sorting through his thoughts. "How long was I out?"

"About fifteen minutes." Leo slid his hand up Jerry's chest to cradle his jaw. He used the hold to get Jerry to turn his head. When they're gazes clashed, Leo grinned. "Of course, driving you unconscious with bliss" — he winked — "definitely a stroke to my ego."

Jerry laughed softly. "I bet." He glanced down at himself. "You already cleaned me up?"

Not only were all traces of the seed he's spilled on himself gone, but his groin and thighs felt dry.

"I did." Leo nuzzled his neck, licking and suckling gently.

"I wanted you to be comfortable when you woke."

Clenching his chute experimentally, Jerry realized he felt stretched in a way he'd never before imagined. He liked it. He also liked the fact that he could feel Leo's seed shifting inside him when he clenched and released, telling him he still carried something of the man with him.

"Thank you, Jer," Leo whispered into his ear.

Jerry turned his attention back to Leo. Seeing the sincerity in the shifter's eyes, he smiled at him. He wiggled a little in Leo's hold, moving to his back, then he wrapped his arms around Leo's neck.

Pulling at Leo, Jerry enjoyed how his lover allowed him to draw him close. He pressed a kiss to Leo's lips, then skimmed his right hand into the shifter's thick hair. Tugging gently, Jerry used the hold to put a little space between their faces so he could focus more fully.

"Thank you, too, Leo," Jerry whispered. "You're an amazing man. Patient. Kind. Loving." He sighed deeply, doing his best not to give in to the feeling that he didn't deserve the man. "You've done so much for me, and I'll never be able to repay that, but I want to spend my life with you trying."

Leo teased his fingertips down Jerry's throat, then rubbed across his torso. "You're a gift, baby. Never think otherwise."

Jerry massaged Leo's scalp, enjoying the intimate touches. "Good thing I feel the same about you."

Easing down on his left arm, Leo cradled both their heads on his arm, clutching Jerry intimately. He rubbed along his ribs and over his hip with his other hand. Tracing lightly over Jerry's skin, he seemed content just to explore him.

Sighing, Jerry cuddled against the man, deciding to do a little exploring of his own. He traced Leo's strong lines, mirroring the other man's touches. Where Jerry was lean and lightly toned, Leo was broader with thicker muscles. Leo had a smattering of chest hair but would never be considered a bear. Jerry found he enjoyed threading his fingers through it.

After several minutes of companionable silence, Jerry wondered, "So where do we go from here?"

"What do you mean?"

Jerry focused on Leo, smiling upon seeing the contented, drowsy look on his face. "I just mean . . . are we living together here? Or—" He paused, nibbling his bottom lip, recalling that the place was a rental. "I guess you have a home elsewhere, huh?"

"Yes to us living together." The lethargic look on Leo's face vanished. "If you didn't realize that, I guess I didn't do a good enough job explaining what it means to be bonded to a shifter."

"Oh, well, you did," Jerry quickly countered. They'd talked about it quite a bit that first day, but—"I didn't want to presume, was all. I don't want to be a mooch." He frowned a little as he thought about that. "I was thinking about getting a part-time job. And my GED. I didn't finish high school, and I'd really like an education, but I didn't want you to think I wasn't grateful. I—"

"Whoa, easy, baby." Leo lifted his forefingers to Jerry's lips, pressing lightly to stall his verbal diarrhea. "The simple answer is . . . I will support you in your goals, and you could never be a mooch." Sliding his fingers up Jerry's nose, he massaged over his eyebrow, perhaps attempting to ease Jerry's scowl lines. "I have a home in the woods halfway between Stone Ridge and Colin City. We can look at the place in the next day or so, and if you like it, we'll move there." Leo shrugged, his expression relaxing again. "If you like this place better, that's fine, too. I can use our time out here to create a new identity for me. It's a little early, but not terribly so."

"New identity. What's that mean?" Jerry asked curiously. He vaguely recalled Leo saying something about creating identities when he'd first met him, but he'd been so scared and stressed out, Jerry couldn't remember much.

"Well, since shifters live around five hundred years, give or take, every few decades we have to either move or hide from society for a decade until those few humans who know us well will forget us."

Leo began rubbing his hands over Jerry's torso again, skimming his fingers down until he reached his dick. Cradling Jerry's cock, he gently rubbed over his softened flesh, causing him to suck in a harsh gasp as his blood began to heat once more.

"Oh, god," Jerry whispered, a tremble working through him as his prick began to swell in Leo's hold. "That should not be possible."

Leo waggled his brows playfully. "Told you we'd be going for hours."

Jerry whined as he stared down at Leo playing with him. His touch was gentle, obviously knowing that, while his penis responded, the skin was extremely sensitive. When Leo slid his fingertips down to tease around his balls, Jerry spread his legs, silently encouraging the touch.

"Talking time over?" Jerry asked as his breath became a pant.

Leo chuckled, his expression full of mischief. "We can keep talking, darling." He rubbed his forefinger over the sensitive patch of skin behind Jerry's balls. "I just couldn't help but explore your beautiful body . . . all spread out and on display for me." Leaning closer, Leo pecked a kiss to his lips, then whispered against them, "You're just too irresistible."

Moaning, Jerry muttered, "Explore away."

Leo did just that.

89

Chapter Eleven

Having pleasured and fucked Jerry until they collapsed sated and exhausted in bed during the wee hours of the morning, Leo shouldn't have been awake. He held his mate close and breathed slowly, listening to the sounds around him. Frowning, he tried to figure out why his wolf was restless in his mind.

Then he heard it. The soft crunch of snow under . . . a booted foot, perhaps?

What the hell?

Leo wasn't expecting anyone. Easing away from his warm mate, he padded naked to the window. Without moving the curtain, Leo swept his gaze over the yard.

The bright gibbous moon lit up the area, giving his excellent shifter vision plenty of light to see by. He checked out the tree line and shadows, figuring out where everything was. After a moment, Leo almost thought he'd been mistaken.

Then he spotted him.

Someone stood just to the right of the woodshed, nearly hidden from view. As Leo watched, the man made some kind of hand movement. In response, four men separated from the trees and began stealthily creeping toward the house.

Leo made out the fact that each carried a handgun.

"Shit," Leo grumbled. "Who the fuck are you?"

His muttered words roused Jerry, who rolled over in bed and peered at him. "Leo?"

"We have company." Leo wasn't going to sugarcoat the issue or coddle his mate. The only way to stay safe was through knowledge. "I count five, and they have guns."

Keeping an eye on the advancing intruders, Leo still saw the way Jerry tensed in his peripheral vision. "Come here, sweetie." He lifted his hand, palm up, and beckoned to him.

Jerry immediately obeyed, scrambling across the bed and joining him, plastering himself to Leo's side.

Leo wrapped his arm tightly around his mate, rubbing up and down his side soothingly. Seeing two men head toward the front of the house and two go toward the back, Leo scowled.

"Lean over and hand me that phone, baby, then get dressed in warm clothes."

To Leo's relief, Jerry did as he was told without question.

Leo took the phone and hit two on speed dial. On the second ring, his alpha answered. "Leo? What's wrong?"

Alpha Declan's curt question didn't surprise Leo. After all, there were few good reasons to call someone at four-thirty in the morning.

"I have at least five men with guns converging on the house. Any news from Jared and Carson as to why that would be?"

"Shit. No. Lark, call Dixon. Tell him to get to Leo's cabin asap." Declan returned to his call, saying, "Dixon's only a mile from you, Leo. And we'll be right behind him. Can ye hold them off until then?"

"Damn straight, I will," Leo grumbled, hearing the sound of movement through the line as well as hearing Lark talking in the background.

"Good. Others will be there soon."

The line went dead, and Leo held the phone out to a fully dressed Jerry. "Take the phone. It's on silent, but if it rings, feel free to answer. Plus, you can use it as a flashlight, if you'd like," he assured, taking Leo's hand and leading him through the house. "Upstairs."

"Aren't you getting dressed?" Jerry whispered the question. His brows furrowed as he kept glancing at Leo's naked form. "You're gonna face 'em naked?"

"One, it'll shock the shit out of them," Leo replied honestly, waggling his brows. "Two, if I need to shift, I can do it faster when I don't have to worry about clothes."

"Oh. Right." Jerry nodded, appearing to understand. "Where will I be?"

Leo saw the way his mate glanced around uncomfortably. They hadn't been upstairs at all. There hadn't been a reason. Still, Leo knew where he was going, even if Jerry didn't.

"In the second bedroom on the left here," Leo told him, guiding him into the room. "The attic door is in the closet. You climb up in there." As he crossed the room, he yanked the blanket from the bed. "If anyone other than me appears, you hide amidst whatever crap you can find up there. Got it?"

To the best of Leo's knowledge, there were a number of boxes stored up there from when he and Luther had cleaned out his parents' home. Leo hadn't had room in his house to store them. Not to mention he just hadn't had the heart to go through them then, so he hadn't minded putting them somewhere else.

An out of sight, out of mind type thing.

"I can't let you face them alone," Jerry objected, dragging his feet. "What if you need me?"

Leo rested both his hands on Jerry's shoulders and stared deep into his mate's pale green eyes. "Jerry, I *do* need you. I need you *safe*." Even as he saw his mate's mutinous look, he told him, "My sweet mate, you are the love of my life. My heart beats for you. Please, I beg of you." Sliding his left hand up, Leo gently massaged his scalp. "Please go into the attic and stay safe."

While Jerry's scent betrayed his displeasure, he still nodded. As he did, Jerry gripped Leo's biceps. "I love you, too. Don't get hurt."

Even knowing it so wasn't the time for their declarations, they still made Leo's heart soar. He dipped his head and plastered a hard kiss to Jerry's lips. Breaking the kiss just as quickly—otherwise, he knew he would get distracted—Leo squeezed Jerry's shoulder, then led him to the closet.

The huge walk-in space was shared with the bedroom on the other side.

Cupping his hands and placing them on his bent knee, Leo tipped his chin up, indicating the hatch in the ceiling. "Step up, grab that ring, and pull down the ladder."

Jerry rested his hand on Leo's shoulder, then placed his left, socked foot into the cradle created by his hands. Resting his weight on Leo, he reached up with his free hand. Jerry grabbed the ring and pulled, but the hatch didn't budge.

"Keep hanging onto it," Leo urged. Shifting his hands, he kept Jerry's foot cradled in one of them. With his free hand, he gripped his hip. "I'm gonna pull you down," he whispered in warning. "Don't worry. I won't let you fall."

With their combined weight, they managed to get the hatch's ladder pulled down.

Leo winced at the sound of the creaking hinges and grinding wood, but it was too late now. He handed the blanket to Jerry, then bounded up the ladder. Once Leo had taken a quick look around and not finding any sign of critters, he returned to the floor.

After cupping Jerry's face and pecking one more kiss to his lips, Leo ordered, "Up you get. And don't worry. Reinforcements will be here in minutes. All I have to do is keep them chasing their tails." Leo winked, hoping he sounded a hell of a lot more confident than he felt.

It'd been a long damn time since he'd faced off against anyone in such a manner. For his mate's safety, though, Leo would rip out the throat of every fucking one of these guys.

As Jerry climbed the ladder, Leo advised, "Head to your left. The wood flooring is thicker, and there are racks of clothes against the back wall, just in case you need more warmth . . . or to hide behind them." As much as Leo hated offering that bit of advice, he knew it was a possibility. "Don't come out until you see me or someone else you know."

Jerry paused and peered down at him, his expression pained. Still, he nodded. A second later, he was gone.

Leo lifted the ladder and closed the hatch. Then he closed the bedroom door they'd come through before slipping out of the far side of the closet. He closed that door behind him as well.

Slinking to the bedroom door, Leo paused and listened. He heard a very faint crunching noise. Frowning, he realized it was someone stepping on a few leaves that had fallen off the logs he'd carried in. That was in the back foyer.

Okay. At least, the back two have gotten inside.

The sound of quiet scraping followed by a click came next, and Leo knew the front door had just been picked.

Damn. I'd hoped to be back downstairs when they got in. At least this way I can stay between them and my mate.

While the humans' steps were light, Leo's shifter hearing could still easily make them out. He crept to the top of the stairs and crouched at the landing, waiting and watching. From his vantage point, he could see down the stairs to the front door as well as between the wooden railing slats and into the living room and kitchen.

As Leo watched, the men in the front room motioned to the pair that were coming in the back. The open floor concept to the right side of the house made that easy. The left side of the home—both upstairs and down—were the bedrooms and bathrooms.

While the pair at the back headed toward the downstairs hallway, the ones who'd come in through the front door headed up the stairs.

Leo eased backward, then slipped into the first bedroom on the left. With the way the furniture was set up, the door would slam into the dresser. Taking advantage of the vacant space between the dresser and the door, Leo peered through the crack created by the swing of the hinges and waited.

As soon as he spotted the first guy slinking into the room, gun at the ready, Leo moved. He slammed the door into the human with as much force as his shifter strength gave him. The stranger bounced off the doorjamb. While he dropped the gun, he also let out a surprised cry.

In an instant, Leo was around the door and grabbing the man's shoulders. He slammed the already dazed human against the wall. Not giving him a chance to recover, he gripped the guy's head and twisted.

The sick sound of popping echoed in Leo's ears. Before he could even let go of the man, the soft *thwack* noise of a suppressed gun being fired sounded through the quiet darkness . . . right before a bit of wood splintered near his left shoulder. Leo shoved the dead man at his counterpart, then followed him, using the human's body as a shield.

Lowering his shoulder, Leo slammed into the dead guy's back, driving him into the live one. The intruder screamed, "Up here," before he went down. Leo pounded his fist into his face, shutting him up and breaking his nose in the process.

"Barney?" someone from downstairs called. "Position!"

Glaring first at the unconscious man as well as the dead guy on top of him, Leo called back, "Barney's not available. Leave now, and I won't kill you."

"Can't do that, asshole," the guy who'd called for Barney

replied. "You got somethin' of ours. We want it back."

Leo rolled his eyes. "What the hell is up with you guys calling young men its? Don't you care that they're people, too?"

"Fags always want their hole filled, so who gives a shit if *we* get paid for it?" a second guy jeered, his tone cutting. "Are you a fag, too? Is that why you're protecting our property?" The stranger chortled cruelly, then he seemed to be talking to the first guy. "Let's take 'em both in. Whadda ya say? If we can't use him, I bet Larson could tell us who would buy him."

Leo gritted his teeth. These guys knew Larson. He was the shifter who'd kidnapped and sold Stephani and Sara to the Robles gang in the first place. While Leo didn't know if this group were gangbangers, if they knew anything about Larson, Leo needed to take as many of them alive as possible.

"Damn," Leo grumbled under his breath.

After Leo heard the first guy agree to take them both, the man spoke into some kind of walkie talkie or microphone. "Got a problem. They were awake, and Barney and Garth aren't responding." He paused a second, evidently listening to a response, for then he answered, "They're holed up on the second floor." There was another pause, then, "Got it." His next comment must have been to his partner, for he stated, "Grab that timber there. We're gonna light the place up and smoke 'em out."

"Oh, fuck no," Leo grumbled. No way was he going to let these assholes torch his grandfather's cabin.

Deciding safety overrode his need to keep as many dudes alive as possible, Leo shifted. He'd just finished the twenty-second transition—give or take a few seconds—when he heard the unmistakable sound of a wolf's howl . . . and it was close.

Fuck yeah. Beta Dixon is here.

Galloping as swiftly as his paws would go as he scrabbled

on the hardwood floor, Leo bolted out the bedroom door. He bounded down the short hallway and lunged, soaring over the stair railing and angling his body at the guy peering into the fireplace. Evidently, the asshole hadn't found a piece that he could pick up, seeing as the embers were low, so he'd been trying to spark up the flames a bit with a large piece of kindling.

Leo took all that in at a glance as his body arced through the air. The other guy shouted, but he ignored it. He also ignored the *thwack, thwack* of another suppressed gun firing wildly toward the ceiling. Leo took courage in knowing that Jerry was hiding at the other end of the house.

With a loud snarling growl, Leo landed on the shocked guy. He wasted no time in wrapping his jaws around the man's shoulder and tearing into the flesh there. At the same time, he dug his claws in and used his impressive wolf weight to flip the guy to the ground.

There was a loud crack as Leo felt his own body slam into the tiles of the hearth. Ripping his jaw away, tearing muscle, flesh, and bone, he released his prey. He bolted toward the kitchen, using the sofa as cover.

To Leo's relief, even as he heard the human who'd been shooting call out, "Daton, you okay? Daton?" the click of a trigger without the resulting *thwack, thwack* told Leo that the guy's gun was empty.

Taking advantage, Leo leaped over the back of the sofa. As he landed on the cushion, he took in the scene. Either the asshole had cracked his skull open on the stones of the hearth and died, or he'd been rendered unconscious. He wasn't moving. Changing direction, Leo used the bounce of the cushion to springboard him at the other final guy . . . who still seemed in shock that he was being attacked by a huge wolf and continued to pull the trigger of his empty gun.

Morons, all of them.

Slamming into the human, Leo took him down with the weight of his big wolf. He wrapped his jaws around the guy's arm and, as he landed, used the momentum to whip the gunman over and around. The move caused the flesh and muscle of the man to tear, and a scream of pain rent the air. Leo lunged forward again, wrapping his jaws around the man's throat.

"Leo, hold!"

Declan's roared order stayed Leo's instinct to clench his jaw and tear out the kidnapper's throat. Still, he shuddered with the temptation. He was onboard with his wolf. Leo wanted to remove the threat to his mate so fucking badly.

Unfortunately, Leo couldn't go against the order of his alpha.

Leo let him go.

CHAPTER TWELVE

Sitting on his butt—and the blanket—with his arms wrapped around his shins, Jerry listened to the thuds, shouting, and eventually, the snarls. He gritted his teeth and rocked forward and back. All the while, Jerry mentally prayed to any god that cared to listen that Leo would be safe.

Did shifters have gods?

Jerry recalled Leo talking about Fate and how he believed that She had chosen them for each other. Deciding She was as good as any—since he thought the god his parents believed in was bogus—Jerry prayed to her. If Fate had brought him to Leo, surely She wouldn't allow them to be torn apart after such a short time together.

With that idea fixed firmly in his mind, Jerry did his best to listen to what was going on beneath him. Things had quieted. Had he missed something?

Then footfalls thudded swiftly up the stairs. A nearby bedroom door slammed open even as he heard Leo order, "Can we get these guys out of here before Jerry sees?"

"Sure, Leo," a deep voice rumbled that Jerry didn't recognize. "Manon, Carson, get these guys out of here. Jared, take care of the guys downstairs with Kade and Mishka."

"With pleasure," Jared's amused voice replied. "I see some fun times in my future."

"Only you would think interrogating guys is fun," Leo grumbled, a low snarl in his voice. "And I still think you're an asshole for putting my mate in harm's way."

"We would never have allowed Jerry to be taken from you," Carson stated, his deep voice holding a hint of annoyance. "Besides, as a shifter, you can survive a bullet wound or two."

"Guys, that's enough," Alpha Declan snapped, a low growl announcing that they were drawing closer. "Carson, you and I are going to have a talk about picking up some of your mate's more dangerous habits. Because when I said Jared had free rein in taking these guys down, this is *not* what I meant."

"Yes, Alpha," Carson replied, his voice even.

Oh, thank you, Fate!

Jerry almost started toward the trap door. Except, he remembered his promise to stay put until he saw Leo. With bated breath, he listened to the movement below. His heart pounded in his chest.

Then . . . there he was.

"Leo!" Jerry jumped to his feet, nearly forgetting to duck so he didn't smack his head on the sloping ceiling.

"Hi, baby," Leo greeted, grinning at him as he held out a hand. "Come on. Time for us to check out that other house I was telling you about." Leo cast a scowling look down the hole he had climbed halfway through. "There's some guys here that are going to give this place a very thorough cleaning."

Jerry eased forward, holding the comforter tight around him. Making it to the steps, he'd never been so happy to have someone wrap his arms around him. He gripped his lover's hand as he pressed into his shifter's side and made his way down the stairs.

At the bottom, Alpha Declan stood in the closet as did a guy he didn't recognize — a big, huge fair-featured dude who was naked. Jerry couldn't help but gape as he swept his gaze up and down the male. The man didn't seem offended, even though he did snap his fingers and wiggle them in an upward manner.

"Up here, little one," the stranger said, clearly teasing as his blue eyes danced with mirth.

Snapping his focus to the man's face, Jerry whispered, "S-Sorry."

"I'm Beta Dixon, and don't sweat it." Dixon grinned, showing off a mouthful of straight white teeth. "I understand you're new to shifter ways, so you'll get used to the nudity before too long."

Jerry was busy nodding absently when Alpha Declan reached out and touched his shoulder. "Are ye all right, Jerry? Injured?"

Quickly shaking his head, Jerry murmured, "Oh. No, I'm good." He turned his attention to Leo as he snuggled closer to his side . . . which was when he realized his mate was still naked. Growling softly, he whipped off his blanket and wrapped it around Leo. "But I'm not used to you flashing everyone, yet, so . . . wear this."

"Of course, baby," Leo immediately responded, tightening the blanket around his waist. With his other hand, he grabbed Jerry and pulled him back against his side, then dipped his head and nuzzled the crook of Jerry's neck. "It'll take time. Just like anything else."

Nodding, Jerry accepted that. He also appreciated that Leo understood he wasn't there, yet. To that end, Leo put himself between Jerry and Dixon's swinging bits.

"Thank you for coming, Beta Dixon," Leo said, looking at him. Then he smiled at Jerry. "Dixon took out the fifth guy who'd been standing watch outside." He huffed a sigh as he shook his head. "I guess Carson and Jared let drop where you were so they could draw out people associated with an asshole named Larson."

Jerry nodded, understanding. "Oh. The shifter who kidnapped your girls." Grimacing, he muttered, "I hope you get your answers from these guys." Remembering the scolding the alpha had given his enforcer, he grimaced as he focused on the head shifter. "It was a good plan, but it sure would be nice not to have to keep worrying about these guys."

"In town, closer to other shifters, we won't have this issue," Leo told him. Nuzzling Jerry's cheek and neck again, he continued by whispering, "There'll even be more people around to give riding lessons to."

Gasping, Jerry gaped at his lover. "H-How did you know?"

In his heart of hearts, in his dreams, Jerry longed to share his love of horseback riding and horses with others. He just hadn't thought he had much of a chance. It was a shock to realize that Leo had picked up on his unspoken dreams.

"Well, I haven't ridden in a coon's age," Dixon commented, crossing his arms over his impressive pale chest. "When you get your stable up and running, I'll be there."

Jerry felt his breath hitch in his chest. Tears stung the backs of his eyes. These people—these shifters—they were so very supportive—more supportive than any people he'd ever met before.

For the first time in almost nine years, Jerry felt like he actually had a family again.

"Thank you." Jerry whispered the words as he grinned around at everyone. Just as ten minutes before, he had been nearly scared beyond belief, suddenly, he'd never felt such welcoming companionship and hope. His cheeks heated as he pressed into Leo's side, loving the feel of his shifter's arm around him. "You guys have made my life worth living again."

"Speaking of making your life better, I actually got you a gift to apologize for putting you in danger." Jared appeared, leaning against the closet doorway. Carson stood behind him with his arm slung low around his waist. Jared winked at Dixon. "Nice dick, Beta, but not as good as my man's." Even as the big male growled, Jared turned back to Jerry. "Head to Frankie and Vince's in the morning. I arranged for your gift to be left with them . . . for safe-keeping."

Dixon heaved a deep sigh. "Gods, you were right, Alpha," he grumbled. "He does take getting used to."

Alpha Declan's chuckle held a wealth of longsuffering.

Too intrigued by Jared's comment, Jerry asked, "What are you talking about."

The lean human winked at him, saying, "You'll see." Then he focused on Alpha Declan. "I came to apologize personally . . . and to tell you that the only reason Carson agreed was because he's my mate, and I told him it would make me happy."

Growling, Alpha Declan curled his lip as he scowled at Jared. "Then I suppose we *all* need to have a talk about not abusing the mate bond."

Jared's cheeks took on a pinkish hue, and he even bowed his head. "It won't happen again," the human stated.

Realizing he would need to ask Leo about the interaction later, Jerry made a mental note. How could someone abuse the mate bond? He wanted to know so he would never put Leo in some kind of tough spot like Jared did to Carson.

"Time to go, baby," Leo murmured into Jerry's ear. "I don't know about you, but I'm ready for sleep." He growled softly before adding, "And winner's sex, because I totally took out those four douche bags who came in here."

More than on board with that, Jerry nodded emphatically.

Unfortunately, by the time Jerry reached Leo's home, he could barely keep his eyes open. Leo had to practically carry him into the home. A few minutes later, Leo had stripped him of his clothes, tucked him into bed, and curled up around him.

Jerry was asleep in seconds.

Gasping, Jerry groaned, reveling in the feel of Leo's erection sliding in and out of his chute. He clenched spastically around his lover's member. Gripping Leo's forearms where they were wrapped around his torso, Jerry did his best to move with his mate's ruts.

Jerry's blood boiled, surging through his veins. He shuddered and trembled in Leo's grip, crying in pleasure when his shifter's dick rubbed over his prostate over and over. Moving his hips, Jerry did his best to meet each of Leo's thrusts, savoring the delicious stretch and feeling of fullness.

"Leo!" Jerry cried, his balls pulling tight, his orgasm threatening. "Please!"

"Yeah, baby," Leo growled into his ear. He lowered one hand and wrapped it around Jerry's prick. "Do it, my sweet. Come for me. Squeeze my cock with your pleasure."

With the way Leo rutted into him coupled with how he jacked his dick, Jerry had no choice. His orgasm swelled as his cock throbbed. In the next instant, he shot, screaming Leo's name as his senses sang with ecstasy.

Jerry shuddered and twitched in Leo's hold. He did his best to squeeze his rectum, and when he felt his shifter's hot seed flood his channel, Jerry let out another moan of bliss. There was something about pleasing his lover that was almost better than his orgasm.

"Oh, Jerry," Leo rumbled. "So perfect. So amazing."

Panting softly, Jerry mumbled, "Yeah it is." Turning his head so he could peer over his shoulder, he grinned at Leo. "Every time with you just gets better. Awesome."

Leo captured Jerry's lips, thrusting his tongue deep. As his man explored his mouth, slowly, Jerry relished every touch, every glide of his fingers and tongue. His arousal began to heat him again.

A loud beep began sounding through the room.

Suddenly, Leo tore his lips from Jerry's, a groan emanating from him. "Fuck! We can't start up again." He leaned over and grabbed his phone. "Shit, it's late. Good thing I set the fucking alarm clock." Leo slowly eased his softening prick out of Jerry's channel even as he nuzzled Jerry's neck. "Sorry, baby. We really need to get up and go."

Jerry moaned, his mind filling with a mixture of annoyance and lust. Scowling at Leo, he mumbled, "Why? What's going on?"

Leo chuckled. "In the future, I'll make certain you get enough sleep, but come on, my love." He slipped from the bed, then pulled back the comforter. Patting a soft smack to Jerry's ass, he urged, "Shower and dressed."

Grumbling under his breath, Jerry did as he was told. He eased from the bed and stumbled to the ensuite shower.

Almost forty minutes later, Jerry had never been so excited for waking up early. He stared through the windshield at the horse inside the fenced enclosure. As soon as Leo parked the truck, he slipped from it.

Jerry jogged to the fence, unable to help himself. He peered across the paddock. His breath caught in his throat, and his eyes burned.

Sensing Leo joining him at the fence—along with Vince and Frankie—Jerry glanced between the smiling group of guys. "It's Jericho."

"Yeah." Frankie grinned broadly, the happy shifter radiating relaxed joy. "When Jared told us you were separated, and he bought him for you, we were happy to offer him a place." The wolf held out a half-full bag of baby carrots. "Go say *hi*."

Grinning broadly, his heart swelling, Jerry murmured his thanks as he took the bag. He turned and gave Leo a hard kiss, then climbed between the fence's slats. As he approached the horse that he'd spent more time with than his parents, Jerry realized that, between the animal and the people standing at the fence line talking softly and smiling at him, Jerry had everything he could possibly need.

Love, family, and acceptance.

Iago's eyes gleamed behind his gold-rimmed frames. "I-I want to go home."

Lindemere sighed. "I'm sorry. Of all the things you would wish for, that's the one I cannot yet grant." After releasing Iago's hand by placing it back on the human's blanket-covered thigh, he slid his hand to his amina's knee and squeezed reassuringly. "But that will not be for all time."

Easing from the bed, Lindemere rose. "Would you care for a meal? You must be hungry after sleeping for so long."

Iago stared up at him, his lips parting a bit. He swept his gaze up and down Lindemere's frame. His shoulders tensing anew, he nibbled his bottom lip.

The scent of unease intensified, tickling Lindemere's sensitive nostrils with its pungent aroma.

"Please." Lindemere took a step backward, offering Iago a bit of space. "I will feed you and share all the answers to your other questions."

Iago's expression of distrust was clear on his face, causing a pang of sadness to spike through Lindemere.

Trying again, Lindemere offered, "I'll build a fire in the fireplace. The front room is comfortably appointed. You could relax and watch me work. Ask me anything, and I' answer honestly."

Swallowing hard enough to cause his Adam's apple to bob along the slender column of his neck, Iago finally nodded once. "O-Okay."

Pleased by his amina's acceptance, Lindemere grinned. "Are you well enough to stand? Or should I carry you?" While Lindemere understood that it was Iago's wrist that was sprained, not his ankle, he wasn't certain if his extended sleep had removed all residual effects of his human crossing through the mist barrier between realms.

"I think I can walk," Iago claimed.

Iago kept a wary eye on Lindemere as he eased to the side of the bed. When he went to grip the comforter with his right hand, he hissed, quickly tucking that hand against his chest. Lindemere took a step forward, his instincts urging him to assist, but Iago's scowl stayed his action.

Except, when Iago went to stand, his knees buckled, a cry escaping him.

Seeing his amina begin to fall, Lindemere lunged forward and swept him into his arms. He cradled Iago to his chest, wrapping his wings around him protectively. Ignoring the way his human tensed, holding himself stiffly in his arms, Lindemere strode from the bedroom.

"You asked what happened, why you were sleeping for a day," Lindemere murmured, needing to fill not only the silence, but to uphold his end of their deal. "Do you remember the fight in the warehouse? When the Four Horsemen fought against the guards holding the paranormals prisoner? My master and his brothers freed me as well as the others. Do you remember that?"

"I remember a group interfering with our work and stealing our test subjects."

Lindemere grimaced upon hearing Iago's belligerent tone. Damn. This is going to be harder than I thought. Sighing he settled Iago on the hide-covered sofa to the left of the fireplace. With the drapes drawn over the windows, the area was cast in shadows, so Lindemere headed to the dining space and lit an oil lamp.

Glancing over his shoulder, Lindemere commented, "Yes, well, those four guys were my master, Death and his brothers, Famine, War, and Pestilence." He saw the way Iago narrowed his eyes, his expression still disbelieving. "Someone cannot just kidnap a demon without consequences."

Iago's jaw clenched, the muscle there flexing.

When he still didn't respond, Lindemere sighed and crossed to the hearth. "Anyway, during the fight, you picked up a gun from one of the fallen guards. I can only assume you intended to shoot at one of the horsemen. Not a wise decision, by the way." He busied himself building a fire, coaxing the purple flames to life with practiced moves. "My master's human lover took exception to that and stopped you."

In his mind, Lindemere winced, remembering his amina's fear-filled cry and the sound of his wrist slamming against the corner of a cage. It'd caused his heart to skip a beat in his chest and rage unlike anything he'd ever felt before to flare within him. Only Death's order to release him had stopped Lindemere from eviscerating Daren.

Once the flames caught, Lindemere turned back to face Iago, taking in his tight form, how his arms were tucked around himself, and the mutinous scowl on his face.

What will it take to get through to him?

"Anyway, I don't know if it was pain or shock, but you passed out. As you are my amina, I brought you here to rest and heal." Lindemere rose, heading toward the food preparation area. After lighting a lamp there, too, he added, "It can be hard on a human the first few times they cross through the mist barrier and into another realm, so I think that, combined with the injury and shock, is why you slept for nearly a day."

Lindemere waited for that to sink in, reaching down and opening the food storage pantry under his home.

"What's an amina?"

Turning, Lindemere focused on Iago. With his heart hammering in his chest, he explained, "When a demon is created by the gods, they are assigned to one of the four horsemen. After completing one thousand years of service, the gods grant us an amina, a person who will be our partner for eternity by bonding their soul with our essence. For me, that person is you."

About the Author

Charlie started writing fantasy when she was eight, and after stumbling onto her first erotic romance at age nineteen, she realized her true calling. She now focuses on writing gay erotic romance, normally of the paranormal variety, with heroes of all kinds. With the help and support of her husband, Charlie finally fulfilled one of her life-long goals . . . move to acreage with her horses. You can often find her curled up with her laptop and a cup of tea or glass of wine, creating her next adventure. Charlie enjoys exploring the mountains of her new Oregon home on horseback, 4-wheeler, or motorcycle.

She can be reached at ch.richards2010@yahoo.com

Or visit her at www.charlie-richards.com